Scribbling and More

Scribbling and More

by

Shirley Young Campbell

A Collection

Mountain State Press
Charleston, West Virginia

International Standard Book Number: 0-941092-32-1

Library of Congress Catalog Card Number: 96-076168

First Edition

Mountain State Press
c/o The University of Charleston
2300 MacCorkle Avenue, SE
Charleston, WV 25304

Printed in the United States of America

Cover Design and Illustrations by Martha Rose Campbell

This is a Mountain State Press book produced in affiliation
with The University of Charleston. Mountain State Press is
solely responsible for editorial decisions.

DEDICATED

Dedicated, with gratitude, to readers, including readers who
have expressed interest in my columns and those who have
decided that publishing this collection is worthwhile, and the
two editors of *The West Virginia Hillbilly* who agreed to let
me fill a corner space in their paper.

ACKNOWLEDGMENTS

The collection of words in this book is the result of a lifetime of scribbling. Long before August, 1991, when the first of these columns was printed, I had written, for other publications, columns which appeared unsigned. My timid submission to Editor Jim Comstock in 1991 was not as timid as similar approaches to other editors in the past. Gratefully, I began writing "Scribbling and More" each week, allowing my name to be printed. I have continued to do so, having recently submitted column No. 203.

Editors Russell McCauley and Jim Comstock have granted permission for reprinting the 113 columns in this book, which first appeared in *The West Virginia Hillbilly*, published weekly at Richwood, West Virginia.

I am grateful to readers Jill Decker, Dagie Gibson and Earl K. Osborne; they have remained faithful and encouraging. I appreciate other readers who have responded specifically to certain columns, such as those which mentioned ants, saltcellars, sayings of Confucius, oiled floors and twinkly mornings.

I am especially grateful to members of my family. Without them, I would have less to say. They have been patient and tolerant. This last statement also applies to Mountain State Press board members who have politely tolerated me.

Shirley Young Campbell,
Charleston, West Virginia
October 23, 1995

NOTE: The cover illustration first appeared in *Hill and Valley* magazine. All illustrations are the work of artist Martha Rose Campbell.

Scribbling and More

☘   August 22, 1991 * ☙

Space in a newspaper is important. Being given an opportunity to have words you have written considered for publication is a privilege, and at the same time humbling. Knowing that your thoughts may be read by many knowledgeable adults produces shyness, at least for me. When I first wrote a column for a weekly newspaper, many years ago, I was so shy that I asked permission to simply call myself a scribbler, and my name was not published.

That column was my first attempt at writing for adult readers. Since that time I have had a few essays, articles and stories published here and there, but my shyness carries over to the extent that I occasionally include apologetic statements explaining that I realize I don't know all the answers to all the questions, and even admitting, at times, that I have failed to see all of my noble ideas produce success. (Editors will sometimes delete such statements, wanting my effort to sound as if I *know* what I am talking about, and not just being wishy–washy.)

* Dates given refer to date published in The *West Virginia Hillbilly*

1

I have now lived long enough to realize fully that I am not nearly so wise or knowledgeable as I thought I was when I first wrote a newspaper column. The fact should improve my offerings–some of which are simply Pollyanna expressions about something to be glad about. (Occasionally I experience such a feeling, even in today's world.)

Sometimes I wax indignant and feel strongly enough about a condition or an event so that I may sound as if I think that if people would only listen to idealists like me the world would be better.

A writing instructor once reminded me that if my ideas or ideals are not quite right, as I feared they might be, that not enough people would agree with me to make a difference, so no harm would be done. And all this reminds me of the fact that the first published poem I was paid for covered a whole page in a magazine and stated chiefly that the world is too full of words! That magazine had a circulation of about 250,000 as I recall. I wonder how many people laughed at me. So be it.

I am grateful to the editor who will consider publishing my ramblings. My self-assigned topic for today was supposed to be more about numbers–statistics, the overwhelming amount of numbers which besiege us, astound us. Listening to budget figures is mind-boggling. Learning that plans for a fleet of planes include the figure of $140,000,000 listed as the cost of each plane is hard for individuals like me to comprehend. I have to concentrate carefully in the grocery store to decide which product is the best bargain. And that thought leads me to thinking of how many people there are in the world, some of them starving.

Looking at pages in *The National Geographic*, or looking at street scenes or news reports on television reminds us of the vast numbers of people who live and breathe on this planet. And then we feel overwhelmed, and can understand a little better why the young people often ask "Who am I?" and "What does it matter?" And yet, each person in the world has fingerprints different from every other person in the world, so we're told, and thus reminded, by writers like Ralph Sockman, that individuals are important and that it is possible for one person to make a difference, even if only occasionally.

❧ August 29, 1991 ☙

We are often surprised, shocked, then bewildered as we see happy carefree children become puzzled, hurt, unhappy young adults. As parents we weathered the months when our children first learned to say "No," and we survived the period when we were often told what other children were permitted to do. We learn to accept and deal with the fact that we were sometimes called unfair. As interested observers we have been prepared by magazine and newspaper articles and by programs on television, even by reading ancient writings, to expect rebellion, occasional moodiness and even depression.

Yet the time may come when we are overwhelmed, when we feel helpless. We know that lifestyles change and try to adjust, but tragedies, crime statistics and knowledge of what has happened to "that young girl" or "that young man" in a community "just like ours" is frightening.

Parents today do not as readily as in the past declare, "Go and darken my door no more," but the tendency is present. Saddened and frustrated because of what has happened to the children we expect to grow up to become perfect adults, we may feel inclined to say, "If you are going to do thus and so, you'll have to leave this house."

The knowledge that knowing nothing is sometimes better than knowing a little and guessing at more tempts us to say, "It might be better if we don't know anything about where you are or what you're doing."

In 1983 a newscaster reported that large numbers of baby calves died as an aftermath of extremely wet weather conditions, because they became so mud–covered that their mothers could not recognize their scent and so rejected them. When we feel like saying, "I'm tired of worrying about you, worn out by being afraid for you," it may be well to remember that we are not parents of calves, but parents and perhaps caretakers of young people, who are, contrary to surface appearances, often bewildered, confused, disappointed, and sometimes, hopeless. We don't understand, they think, and perhaps we should recognize that they, in turn, do not fully understand themselves and the situation they are in, and really don't know how to cope.

Rules and standards are well and good; hopes and moral concerns are important, but parental love is important, too, and the opportunity for the children, the young people, to know that we love them and will help if we can should not be unattainable. They should not be shut out to flounder in the mud, cut off from assistance, rejected and lost.

Even in this "land of plenty" where many of us, not all, have as much as 100 times more to be thankful about than people in some countries, we can find something to complain about. Our complaints, I'm sure, often seem petty. Mine do, some of them, and not important enough to write about in "letters to the editor." I'm usually not adverse to writing to editors, however, and I hope that some of my letters serve a good purpose. My most recent effort pointed out that trains seem to go very fast through a section of town where pedestrians often cross the tracks.

I doubt that the trains have slowed as a result. They are permitted by law to go faster than I had thought, according to information I received, but it does seem to me that I hear train whistles more often, and this is good if it's a fact, and not my imagination. (The engineers may be just tooting in my vicinity to remind me that I didn't know what I was talking about when I mentioned having heard that trains are sometimes limited to 30 miles an hour in towns.)

Some of my petty complaints prompt me to use column space to air them. I realize that we are blessed with comparatively plentiful water supplies and indoor plumbing. Nevertheless, I want to say –"loud and clear"– that I wish builders and planners would consider carefully the size of toilet stalls and the location of accessories within those stalls, and I say this quite seriously. Recently, I was very disappointed in a beautiful new restaurant, that seemed super clean and nicely kept, when I discovered that one of those very large gadgets now being used to cover and keep the tissue sanitary was placed in such a position that I could hardly wedge past it to get the door closed. And I am not

5

extremely overweight; in fact, I am small compared to a few other people. Please–carpenters and plumbers, try entering and closing the door before you strike the final hammer blow or fasten the last of the nuts and bolts.

And another thing, speaking of restaurants–I love'em, love eating out, appreciate the hard work waiters and waitresses do, but I wish some of them could be reminded, as my eighth grade home economics teacher told us long ago, that it is not polite or sanitary to pick up drinking glasses by the tops. Also, I'm always relieved when the pitcher from which a cup or glass is being refilled does not rest on the top of the cup or glass. Maybe this is enough petty complaining to last for a year, but there is one more thing.

Years ago, one of my favorite women's magazines accepted and printed household hints sent in by readers. I wrote to the magazine, probably more than once, saying I wish the wrappers of sticks of butter and margarine would be clearly marked so that I can find the edge of the wrapper in a hurry. My hint wasn't published, but some time after that the wrappers included measurement marks, indicating 1/4 cup, 1/2 cup, etc. This was great and it is helpful, but to this day, it's still difficult to find the edge of the wrapper. So, if anyone who packages margarine or butter happens to read this, please discover what it's like to try to find the edge of the wrapper when it's time for dinner and everything isn't ready. Then perhaps you'll decide to add a helpful marking–an arrow or a line and the words *Open here*.

My peace–making efforts have won no medals. I have not attained fame as a pacifist. Shortly before the bombs began dropping last winter my two urgent letters to an editor were published, but they failed to stop Desert Shield from becoming Desert Storm. As a result, I attempted to enclose myself in a shell. Sixty years of disappointment are enough, I thought.

When I was very young I believed that we were too wise to be led into war by munitions makers. We had been told that this is what happened when our country fought the war to end all wars. My high school assembly speech celebrating Armistice Day emphasized this belief.

In college in the thirties I "chickened out," and didn't mail my letter to the college newspaper. Based on what I heard, I decided my letter would achieve nothing since people around me refused to be wise. They considered war inevitable.

During World War II I found it impossible to remain unemotional when I considered the "Facts" of war. I wanted our country to be safe; I wanted my husband and my brother to come home safely, but I couldn't forget that the enemy included brave men who weren't ready to die. I still believe that intelligent people could somehow find means other than war to solve problems.

After World War II I was busy rearing children, but I ached with sympathy when a small fuzzy–voiced boy asked me why people want to kill each other, and when one of my daughters sent a letter to Russia pleading that people try to get along with each other. I was unhappy in the Vietnam era when protesters were berated and called unwashed bums. I had hoped that people had learned to understand each other.

During the past year I have become aware that writers such as Taylor Caldwell and Gore Vidal are hinting at the possibility that wars, like stock market ups and downs, may be the result of manipulations by selfish individuals and are not the inevitable result of world conditions. I have mentioned this a time or two. Before the Desert Storm cease-fire, and after, I was, to an extent protected by my shell. I made an effort to remain calm, to accept the status quo. I tried to limit the amount of war news I absorbed. I don't like to listen to statistics about planes or tanks or any announcements that seem to ignore the fact that such machines are manned by beings who have been born, lived, hoped, dreamed in the world which we, too, inhabit.

In a small house I could not always ignore the news. Finally, one day, I heard something that shattered my protective shell, but in a way that caused me to be very thankful. A young man, interviewed while working to aid and perhaps save lives of injured prisoners, said, in answer to a question, "They're just human beings, sir, just human beings."

Our country feeds and cares for prisoners and young medics work hard to help. Some small progress is being made in civilization's long upward climb and I am glad.

Last year a magazine editor asked me to write an article about changes in education. She had published a story of mine and learned that I have lived a long time and have had some teaching experience. I wrote an article based on what I read about today's education in books such as *From Socrates* to *Software*, *The Closing of the American Mind* and *The Great School Debate*.

The editor returned the article; she wanted my personal opinion. This was flattering, even though I was aware that my opinions might not be valued by everyone. I complied with her request and now realize that doing so has set me to thinking of some unanswered questions.

I realize I don't know enough about discipline, I think it is probably easier to know what methods will bring the best results in a classroom–far easier–than it is to know how to instill self-discipline in one's own children. We hear much about laxity in rearing children, but there is and always has been a question concerning whether harm can be caused by an overly strict discipline. A teacher must be in control in a classroom, but as parents we have hard decisions to make about loosening control.

We have often heard that military service will do wonders toward developing self-control, otherwise described as "making a man of him," but I have never been in complete agreement with this. If someone is told what to do every minute of a 24 hour day, and forced to do it, how does that develop self-discipline? And yet we must have rules for our children to follow as they grow and see that they follow those rules.

9

*   *   *

As we recall people who have "controlled," or failed to control us in the past, the presence or lack of a certain quality is evident. Influence is often exerted without fanfare, with dignity. (*Hullabaloo* would probably be a more appropriate word here than *fanfare*.) *The West Virginia Hillbilly* readers in the past have read of Professor Lucy Prichard who often provided assistance to struggling college students. I was privileged to work for Miss Prichard at Marshall during my senior year and during that year I made a serious mistake by giving an incorrect meeting date on letters mailed to Latin teachers throughout the state. As I recall, Miss Prichard did not lecture me, telling me I had been careless and must do better. She didn't shout, but merely told me quietly what had happened. I had been the cause of confusion, of late night phone calls, but she didn't "fire" me or fuss at me. Probably all of us can contrast her response to that of naggers or screamers we have known.

*   *   *

I am grateful for telephone service and mail delivery, and sometimes pause briefly, thinking what it would be like to do without a telephone, and imagining how it would seem to have to depend on stage coach or pony express.

&   October 3, 1991   &

The sign said "Economics" and I stopped at the designated table. Discarded library books were on sale. Could I possibly pick up a book that would give me simplified definitions? I looked at a few books hopefully, but soon moved on to another table.

I was enrolled in an economics class long ago, and I also studied political science, but I remember little of what I was supposed to learn in those classes. I have never understood the complexity of international trade, the apparent necessity for controls. I don't understand domestic trade problems, either. It seems to me that buying what you need and selling what you produce could be so simple.

Do authorities try to determine whether imposed controls are fair to everyone? Why are retailers allowed to raise prices immediately when news comes of a freeze that will affect farm products? The produce on the counters has been bought previously at a lower price. I know this is only a minor consideration in a complex system.

Sometimes it seems that no one knows what to do about inflation, recession, depression. Sometimes it seems that the authorities aren't even sure which stage is current. A question raised as commentators discussed the recent coup in Russia and factors preceding the coup caused me to look for explanations concerning balance of trade. I learned little and I'm still pondering. What should we think about the use of food as a weapon of war or a means of persuasion—either by withholding it or using it to extract concessions?

My encyclopedia tells me that sometimes food and medicines are excluded when nations attempt to "persuade" other nations by withholding goods or limiting trade. When such exclusion is not in effect, I suppose we might take comfort in the thought that it is better to have less to eat and fewer bandages to apply–far better–than to be blown to pieces by bombs, but I don't find the thought very satisfactory.

The loaves and fishes mentioned in the Bible come to mind and then I recall that the economics professor often said in his long-ago economics class, "You should always leave the table hungry." And then I think of the fact that tonight I ate an after-dinner snack I didn't need.

In late August I made crab apple jelly. My well-worn cook books, some inherited, tell me that I must not press the juice from the cooked apples if I want the jelly to be clear. After the juice was collected, I discarded the soft apple sections. They would feed several starving people, keeping them alive for a little while.

℣ October 10, 1991 ℣

Surely something can be said about the persistence of life. The tiny, seemingly fragile ants, not much larger than a dot made by a pencil, seem to survive, as a tribe, in spite of smashing, spraying, chasing and all precautions. They invaded our kitchen during the last weeks of summer. They would seem to be gone, and then, lo and behold, a scout appears, lured by a crumb or a spoon someone has left in the sink. Sometimes two scouts appear. Like flies, they are apt in ability to maneuver, evading demolition. They seem to know when a human approaches and scurry madly. They are so tiny and try so hard, I almost feel reluctant to demolish them.

The blades of grass that appear in a crack in concrete on one of the busiest streets in town cause me to contemplate in amazement the persistence of life. In our garden a flower blooms on a plant we thought was lost. The blossom appears on a stem supported only by a plant whose root is on top of the dry hot soil.

A baby smiles through tears, and a "much put upon," handicapped adult survives to build a niche for himself in a respectable, decent position. Life persists.

Somehow, these thoughts lead me to think of ancient buildings, many of which no doubt have survived invasions of ants. Some of them have also withstood enemy invasions and pillaging. Viewing travelogues or reading of ancient cites, we learn of buildings still in use, 400, 700, 900 years old and more. A building in Istanbul, praised as "one of the world's noblest works of architecture," was built 1,454 years ago and, according to my 1975 reference, was still in use when it was 1,437 years old.

As I write this I think of watching the demolition of a building that had walls made, not of one thickness of bricks, but several. A residence, the house was perhaps only fifty years old, but probably was much older since it was so sturdily built. The house, it seemed to me, as I watched from an office window, was in good condition, but someone needed a parking lot. I hope some of the bricks were salvaged.

I searched the encyclopedia for information about old buildings still in use in Europe and Asia, and I found many examples of structures cherished for their beauty or their present-day usefulness, several having survived for more than 1,000 years.

It seems we rather like tearing down buildings in America, thinking we'll build "bigger and better." Perhaps this tendency is a carry-over from log cabin and sod hut days. I hope that the majority of the replacements are safe and stable, not overnight-built structures that won't even withstand rainstorms well.

❧ October 17, 1991 ❧

Recently I had a few minutes' conversation with someone whose book I had read in manuscript form. "What have you done with your book?" I asked, because I remember thinking that the manuscript was well worth publishing, and should not be left on a shelf to turn to dust. The author at first seemed not to realize what I was thinking about. "Oh, that. I haven't done anything with it. I just went on to something else."

To get on with something else that needs doing is good, but good manuscripts, in my opinion, should be treated with persistence. We probably shouldn't take out second mortgages in order to buy postage for mailing manuscripts, but good writing certainly seems worth a few extra stamps.

*   *   *

At the book sale where I failed to find a book of definitions that would help me understand international trade, I purchased several novels, three of them by West Virginia authors. I was somewhat shocked to find that books written by West Virginians had been discarded, but I've enjoyed reading those I purchased. One of the three, *Letter From Peking* by Pearl Buck, is filled with so much love that it brought tears to my eyes, something that does not happen often these days. I find words worth quoting in the final pages: "In the midst of angers and . . . wars love's secret work goes on, and binds us all . . . whether love is denied or love is bestowed."

*   *   *

14

I am sure that James A. Haught's new book, *Science in a Nanosecond*, can be helpful to some members of my family and I bought a copy with that result in mind. The illustrations are helpful, I assume, and the questions are surely similar to those anyone might have asked at some time. They range from such things as What do we see when we look at a rainbow? to What are quasars, white dwarfs and lightning? Also included are more complicated questions such as those related to quarks, DNA, photons and gluons. *

I have spent only a few minutes with the book since I received it and it seems a bit advanced for me, since I was born long before the space age, but I have faith in James Haught's ability. My faith is the result of long acquaintance with his writing for *The Charleston Gazette* and I am still hopeful that I will see the publication in book form of his series of articles on religion.

Regarding my scientific ability, I am basking in the fact that recently, after I heard my youngest grandson tell someone that he isn't sure where the wires go when wind power is used to make electricity, I got busy and gained a smattering of knowledge about generators so that I could explain that it isn't necessary to connect wires to windmills. [It isn't, is it?] I still don't know how radios work, and I'm not sure whether it's easier to close a car door with the window open or shut. I could experiment but I think I'll leave that to someone else.

*Information about Mr. Haught's book may be obtained from "*The Charleston Gazette*" or from *Prometheus Books* in Boston.

I received a call from a friend who says, although she is not very active at present, she has achieved more in the fifteen years since she learned she has cancer than in any other period of her life. She has, however, been an achiever throughout her lifetime. Her accomplishments include adjusting to becoming a citizen of an unfamiliar country and making possible a good life for her daughter.

For several years she has been interested in writing and I am confident that this has helped her. She has had a number of pieces of her writing published and has enjoyed participation in a poetry group. The first writing workshops I have conducted were held in her apartment, due to her beginning interest in writing.

*   *   *

While our learned, nimble-witted editor hurries through transograms and acrostics with involved literary messages, I have only recently learned to do cryptoquips fairly rapidly. These, with their uncomplicated messages, such as "Why do we drive on parkways and park on driveways?" can't begin to measure up to acrostic quotations, but I realize that I must accept my limitations.

*   *   *

In Corpus Christi during World War II on the naval air force base where my brother was to receive his wings as pilot and navigator, I was amused and pleased to see a sign in the women's restroom saying, "Wash your hands before you leave this room," or words to that effect. However, I was sorry to think that young ladies had to be reminded. (The posted sign, as I recall, was so mandatory in tone that I wouldn't have been greatly surprised if someone had been posted outside the door to check for compliance!)

Considering things I've written in previous columns, I think I should mention that the house where I was born had no indoor plumbing. We lived there for four years so I know how to appreciate modern restrooms, even if people need to be reminded to use soap and water.

Incidentally, I attended the commissioning of the USS West Virginia (SSBN 736) in Georgia last fall, and I failed to find a provision for handwashing in the facilities placed for public use. I'm not sure what this tells me about changing times.

*   *   *

The characteristics of West Virginia are still being discussed by sociologists, statisticians, historians, but perceptions have changed a little. We were discovered by outsiders a few decades ago and considered and written about at great length. A recently developed trend I have noticed in fiction annoys me. Instead of describing us as isolated people with quaint customs, writers seem to be identifying problem characters in their stories set in locations outside of West Virginia as people who have migrated from West Virginia.

A novel I started to read recently, written by one of our most prestigious writers, I put aside soon after a very unsavory character, physically dirty and psychologically impaired, was identified as belonging to a family of West Virginia origin. Members of the family had settled in New York. I'll read the book later–I bought it–but I'm not happy about what I've read so far.

❧ October 31, 1991 ☙

At long last I have begun and completed a large part of a task I have merely talked about for years. I am sorting and arranging in order the many books that take up room in our house. Since I'm trying to divide my time among several delayed projects, I usually work only 1/2 hour at a time at book sorting. Most of the books are arranged according to authors' last names, and I noticed as I filled part of a shelf with books written by people whose names begin with a C that a book by Jim Comstock seemed to be resting comfortably next to *The Wisdom of Confucius* and I wondered if I would find other books belonging on the shelf that would be placed between those two.

After several days I had used all the space available in that set of shelves and I had ended with *Germinal* by Zola. It was interesting to note that Comstock and Confucius are still "neighbors" in Section No. 4 of the bookcase.

*   *   *

Two sentences in UNICEF'S latest plea for help: "In the 1980's more than 1.5 million children died as a direct result of war . . . Why is it that the children always suffer most?"

*   *   *

Speaking of scientific knowledge and curiosity– Although I am not in the least eager to learn the many difficult-to-comprehend facts about space travel and interplanetary communication, there are a few modern developments that arouse my curiosity. I would like very much to know how the plastic tablecloths that look like beautifully textured cloth are made. Some of these have intricate patterns and cause me to wonder whether they may be made of cloth and then dipped into or coated with plastic. I admire them, just as I also admire and appreciate any cloth that lets me see the interweaving of threads. Odd, you say? Unusual, perhaps, but then I'm, the person who loves to see the fallen maple leaves that have landed upside

18

down on the grass. I like the way their pale green color complements or blends with the darker green of the late summer grass. I miss the picture they make when the mower puts an end to the leaves or someone rakes them away.

*   *   *

Yesterday I began reading one of the long-neglected books that came to light as I worked at my task of bringing order to our book shelves. Published in 1950, page 44 of the novel has two sentences about commerce that especially interested me. Lawrence Schoonover, author of *The Gentle Infidel*, stated that the "frankly monopolistic" Venetian Renaissance commerce was . . . " inextricably tangled with politics." The story begins in the year 1444.

*   *   *

Sitting in a car parked near a grocery store on a Sunday afternoon, seeing the many kinds of people coming and going, thinking of their problems, the ups and downs of their lives . . . This makes me feel that I am ignorant and presumptuous.

❧ November 7, 1991 ☙

Daniel Webster said, "There is nothing so powerful as truth, and often, nothing so strange." I think the citizens of the United States of America have a right to know everything that happens in sessions of the Senate, and even a right to know everything that every senator says in every meeting of U.S. Senators. An article in the October-November issue of *New River Free Press* states that Dr. John Reuwer said in a speech that although governments will always be necessary, they "need to be directed and chastised . . . by ordinary people courageously standing for their highest principles."

19

Several years ago I wrote an article which said that older people can be an oasis of comfort for younger people. The article was published with an attractive illustration showing an elderly woman rocking a small boy. I think I had two points in mind: Older people need not feel useless and they should not be unhappy because they no longer have an active role in managing family affairs. Probably I had a third "ulterior motive" in mind: Grandparents should not be critical and carping because they don't approve of the way the younger generation members are rearing children.

As the years passed my situation and related thoughts about being a grandmother have altered. Not long ago, comparatively speaking, I wrote an article which said that grandparents can change and adjust to taking care of– again–younger children. That article, perhaps not detailed enough, or maybe not convincing, was sent out a few times and rejected. It has never been published.

It is fairly easy to avoid being in the way and to be an oasis which will help children if that is all that is required of you. However, the situation is different if you are the person who must say "Yes" or "No, you can't" or "Stop that" all day long, five or more days a week. It is easy to think fondly of the pleasure of having a drowsy small child cuddle on your lap. It is difficult to appreciate fully the merits of an eleven-year-old while he faces you defiantly saying, "I don't have to."

Hundreds, perhaps thousands, of grandparents are helping care for children today. It may help us to cope well if we think of alternatives, if we consider all the things that could happen to harm or hurt children if we were not caring for them. We can try to be glad for a "second chance," hoping to help build strength of character and install ideals for children of a third generation. Perhaps, with luck, we can avoid mistakes we may have made rearing our own children. We certainly have no cause to feel useless.

*   *   *

Speaking of truth, Robert Browning said that truth never hurts the teller.

⧞ November 14, 1991 ♋

Arms widespread, ready to offer a welcoming hug, with a broad smile on her face and genuine pleasure reflected in her eyes, my grandmother stood to greet family or friends. In addition, she was ready to serve and entertain in whatever unobtrusive way she could. During all the years when I was privileged to know and love her, she was a widow, and during most of that time, she lived either in my family's home or in her daughter's home. Her patience, dignity and love made her a welcome member of either household. She never intruded, and only once during the years did I hear her utter a word of criticism of family members, and then she whispered a simple expression of regret, chiefly engendered, I think, by the fact that she could no longer take an active part in household chores.

Past eighty at that time, she confided to me that when she had an opportunity she "slipped around" and gathered all of my cousins' socks and washed them by hand. It pleased her to think that she was thus contributing importantly, even though she was no longer permitted to perform heavier tasks. She had worked hard all her life, "working out" as a girl; later, keeping boarders after her husband's death, but performing tasks willingly and cheerfully. I remember her laughing with a measure of

21

chagrin as she recalled an occurrence of years past when she had failed to iron one sleeve of a shirt while she worked as a hired girl in a large household. I am sure she must have been greatly embarrassed by such a failure because I recall seeing her iron clothes painstakingly and carefully, attaining perfection by pinching tiny pleats in ruffles.

Her habit of serving carried over into her later years; she was usually the last person to be seated at the dining table and probably would have been quite willing to stand to serve everyone if asked or permitted to do so. When urged to sit, she would say she wanted to be sure everyone had what was needed. Yet, she was by no means servile or abject; she had the dignity of a queen at times, especially when dressed in her "best," her hair coiled neatly in Eleanor Roosevelt style and her back "ramrod straight," her head held high. She was not envious, but I did hear her mention casually once that she had always thought it would be nice to have a gray silk dress and a gray fur piece to wear with it. Her "widow's compensation" was tiny; she received $20 a month, but often that money was spent on one or more of her grandchildren.

She was uncomplaining. The sorrow and regret I heard her express were for people she read of in the newspaper, especially children who were mistreated. I can see her yet, standing, reading, shaking her head in perplexity and sorrow.

Another picture I have as I think of her shows her sitting patching my father's work clothes, skillfully mending with tiny stitches, enjoying the work. However, in the most vivid recollection, the reality of her love, its warmth and comfort are emphasized, and I see her standing in a doorway or on a porch ready to offer a welcoming hug, expression of her genuine affection.

First, there was the Coles' house high on a hill overlooking the many houses located along a creek and beside the railroad below. I went to their house a few times, either with my mother or my aunt. Mrs. Cole was a pleasant lady. The house was very large and in it a mechanical piano played "I'm Forever Blowing Bubbles." Wild honeysuckle vines twined on the double stairway leading to the front porch. Another house on a hill a short distance away on another branch of the creek looked like a mansion. I have a vague memory of white pillars and yellow exterior.

The hill house I know more about than either of the two I have mentioned was not far from our home on the branch of the creek where we lived. (Readers probably understand that when we said "on the creek" or "up the creek" we didn't mean that we lived *in* the water.) There were many, many steps straight up the hill leading to that house, and I remember that my mother and I went there once, either to return or receive, or lend, the patterns for the doll clothes that my mother made for me. I remember little of the interior of the house that we may have seen when we were there, but I remember some of the doll clothes. Perfectly made, intricate, they followed carefully designs for "people clothes." I remember particularly a little "shirt waist," an undershirt, with buttons added so that undergarments could be buttoned on.

Years later, I went to that house twice. The first time, the important family connected with the patterns for doll clothes still lived there. (The family was important probably because they may have owned or had a large interest in the coal company or because the man of the family was "the big boss.") I was there for a Sunday dinner following a summer camping trip participated in by daughters of the family. I remember the large sunny bedroom where the older daughter shared her poetry scrapbook with me.

Later, I spent an evening during a Christmas holiday in the house. The "very important coal company family" no longer lived there. Times had changed, and a young doctor and his wife lived in that house on a hill. I was home from college for the holiday. A young man who lived near the doctor took me to visit in the large house that had once been so important in the community. I wore a brown velvet dress and we spent most of the evening playing Ping-Pong in a large room that may have been either on the third floor or in the attic of the house.

The next house on a hill that has a prominent place in my memories of coal camp life was in the community where I lived from the time I was nine until I was twenty-two. It, too, had many access steps. The mine superintendent's family lived there. The daughter who was near my age was my "best friend" for many years, so I climbed those wooden steps often, hoping that the family's pet bulldog would not interfere. The thing I admired most about that house was the breakfast room.

Quite often the big houses, the big bosses', were on hills in coal camps. In recent years I have wondered why these houses seem to disappear first when mines are closed, and the small houses clustered below often remain. I think the disappearance that surprised me most was that of the yellow house with white pillars, the house which I had never entered. When we drove through the changed, inactive coal community where it had been I could hardly believe my eyes. Perhaps there are traces or remains that I couldn't see, but it seems that all the coal camp houses on hills, "the big houses," that I have known, have faded away.

❧ November 28, 1991 ☙

Quite, often, it seems that things we wish we could recall more clearly involve little matters, seemingly unimportant to everyone except the individual who is trying to recall the "little thing." I suppose men might wish they paid more attention to the method their fathers used to fix doors that wouldn't close properly, or the procedure used to rid lawns of weeds. Recently, I have been wondering why it is so difficult to prevent dishcloths from looking dingy. For the most part I seem to have good results with my laundry. As I thought of my dishcloth problem, I realized that I cannot recall anything about the dishcloths in my mother's kitchen. I don't remember what they were made of, what they looked like, or how clean they seemed. It's possible that I didn't wash dishes often enough when I was young. However, while sharing cake and coffee with neighbors I asked about dishcloths and was reassured—keeping dishcloths snow white *is* a problem.

    *   *   *

I have learned that men do sometimes read columns written by women. I know, too, that they can be very harsh in their criticism of women's writings, perhaps accusing us of being idealists or sleep walkers who don't know what year this is. I've also learned that a few people will say boldly that they like to read recollections of things past, even if written by women. Such may remind them of days and years that seem golden compared with the present. Incidentally, I haven't learned whether anyone likes or dislikes my scribblings in this paper.

    *   *   *

A change from one season to another seems to create problems at times. My mother was often sad in the fall. I have thought that perhaps this was because she didn't have an opportunity to go to school as many years as she would have liked, but she liked working with flowers and in her vegetable garden, so perhaps this caused her to be melancholy in October. My husband remarked once that finishing with his garden in the fall could be compared to taking down a Christmas tree.

In the past fall has seemed invigorating to me, but this year I seem to be somewhat cranky and crabby as storm windows are installed and flowers are brought into the house. Probably I'm cross because I haven't accomplished everything I would like to have done, and the year is drawing to a close.

My uncle expressed his thoughts about time as he grew older by saying that time is like a stallion that takes the bit in its teeth and runs, taking you faster than you want to go. But, he said, time is also like a pool of quiet water. It stops a while and then moves on, and each drop of water carries a bit of your life with it as it goes.

Perhaps changing seasons emphasize our feelings about time, thus affecting our emotions, but it may be good to recall that it has been said that people accomplish more in countries which have more than one season.

    *   *   *

In a discussion group someone remarked that she had been careful to keep quiet concerning her feelings about a national event because her opinion seemed contrary to that of people around her. A quotation that was one of my favorites in years past admonished us to keep quiet if we have doubts about God or man or self. That may very well be excellent advice concerning religion, but when it comes to government or foreign policy and political maneuvers, it seems to me that it may be good to sound off "loud and clear."

    ❰ December 5, 1991 ❱

I recall hearing my father say that O. O. McIntyre said he could write better when his feet were cold. I haven't noticed that my writing improves in cold weather. In fact, for me it's a little harder to put thoughts on paper when the house is chilly. I've always admired the efforts of people who say they get up at five or thereabouts and write until it's time to go to work or eat breakfast, but I have seldom followed their example.

*   *   *

Thinking of what I said in a previous column about the "right" of every citizen to know everything said by senators in session, I realized that some might say this is wrong because people of other countries shouldn't know what our senators say. Why not? If senators vote to withhold aid to a country, the people of the country will know without being told that they're not receiving aid. News can be delayed, of course, as it often is, "for our protection," but, in my opinion, sooner or later, we, the people, should know exactly what has been said.

*   *   *

Twice recently I have heard television discussions of "friendly fire" war casualties. During one program someone said, "There is nothing new about friendly fire casualties." It certainly seems likely that deaths have occurred because of errors made inevitably in warfare during all the years since armies first formed. Tolstoy's *War and Peace*

definitely emphasizes that confusion can occur as men line up to kill each other.

*   *   *

It has always seemed to me to be rather ironic that we have "rules for war," but since such rules, particularly those regarding prisoners, seem to have promoted a measure of humane treatment, we can be glad when rules are followed.

*   *   *

A manuscript was returned to me with the word *moderately* underlined in a sentence regarding Billy Edd Wheeler's success as a playwright. The editorial reader had placed an exclamation mark in the margin after underlining the word. I think I was right to use the word *moderately* in that particular sentence because Mr. Wheeler's play, *Slatefall*, which I saw years ago, deserves to reach Broadway, but like other plays with coal mining settings, including one written by me and one by Jean Battlo which I have been privileged to read, his play didn't "fly" in New York. Parts of the play were incorporated in a performance in Tennessee recently, and this is good, of course.

My rejected article included this sentence: This is a step forward in efforts to tell a complete coal mining story, but it is sad that the original *Slatefall* languished unseen and unheard for so many years. It seems to me that many people–even people in our state–don't want to listen to anything related to coal and I think this is regrettable. It is not surprising that people often have an incomplete picture of coal miners and their families and the coal mining life.

❧ December 12, 1991 ☙

I have tried to examine with honesty my feelings about coal mining people. I realize that I was fortunate as I grew up in a coal mining community although my father was not an executive; he worked very hard as a mine electrician. My husband was employed as a coal miner at the time of our marriage. He worked on his knees in thirty-inch-high coal.

Life was fairly calm in our community. We knew about the occasional fights, a murder or two, a disrupted household, but I have lived more years outside of the coal mining area than in it, and I have learned that there is as much or more trouble in "respectable, non-mining" areas as in a mining community.

Over a period of many years I have written about coal and coal mining people. I have managed to have my book about coal mining published in my home state and I am grateful for that, but I have come to feel that any story, any play, that touches the subject of coal immediately has a count against it–both outside the state and in it. I realize that this can be construed as an "excuse," a statement of "why I have never become famous."

However, I have been persistent in my efforts to present a positive picture of coal mining people because I am very much concerned about the incomplete story of the coal mining life that has usually been presented with the result that many people have misconceptions about miners and our state.

As always, tragedy and death and trouble are newsworthy, and perhaps people outside of our area cannot be blamed when their knowledge of coal mining is based on such news, but something or someone needs to add to their knowledge, and in my opinion it would be quite desirable if more editors, publishers and producers could be persuaded to do so. I was pleased to see the women in the movie "Matewan" nicely dressed, but I imagine that this might have surprised some of the comparatively few viewers who saw the picture, because they had learned to look for coal-blackened faces.

The "good side" of coal mining life is presentable. Perhaps some day a scene showing coal miners, scrubbed and clean in the evening, loafing near the company store, will be as desirable, seem as acceptable to producers and directors as a chorus of Oklahoma cowboys. Someone may decide that a chorus of coal community neighborhood women singing about love, or having a humorous discussion of mothers' and daughters' relationships, or some such, will seem as interesting as the speeches of members of a chorus line in New York. We can hope that such will occur and continue to try to produce coal mining literature which presents "another facet" of the coal mining story.

❧ December 19, 1991 ❧

SUNLIGHT IN DECEMBER, DECEMBER 22, 1984

The scratches show through the wax, but the wax is shiny.
The sun is bright and the smear marks on the glass
in the front door persist, resisting all my efforts,
but I am not discouraged. I like the sunlight.

I am happy in this house today. One daughter
takes time to help the other.
My husband makes four jars of jam for grown-up children
away from home. I am glad—even though
he put vanilla in the jam—of all things—
obstructing the tangy taste of the blackberries
he picked last summer.

31

I like the sunlight on this shortest day of the year
and the article I read in a magazine I found in the trunk
told of a woman who said, "The sunrise shouts
on Christmas day."

DECEMBER 30, 1984

The Christmas tree still stands, green and gold.
Red and white tokens glitter yet
Around the room, some new, some old.
I sit in the glow.
The only sound I hear,
besides the tell-tale hum in my ear,
is football on TV.
No carols today, no Boston Pops.

Five days since Christmas, and I know
It's time to take it down, since
my husband says it's so.
But I frown, reluctant to see it go.

It's too soon to have Christmas stop.

TAKING DOWN THE TREE , JANUARY 1, 1985

My husband says, "Taking down the tree is like clearing up
the garden in the fall."
I'm glad he said that. I didn't think he would.
I know he feels a sense of loss when the garden season
ends.

❃ December 26, 1991 ❄

It's a sad day when we must tell children we can't
let them "lick the bowl" if the cake batter has raw eggs in it

32

because we have been told that, due to the method of nurturing chickens these days, eggs must be thoroughly cooked for safety. We'll have generations to come in which mothers will never have the delight of listening to two small children arguing happily over who gets the cake batter spoon. Such a mother will never know what it's like to see small faces decorated with chocolate batter. So I think, but being a Pollyanna, I must add that we can be glad somebody out there is thinking about what's in the food we eat and handing out dire warnings.

As I write, I think of the term "sob sister," which was applied to women reporters in the past–possibly because they were only permitted to write obituaries or advice for the lovelorn. No Mary McGrory types in days of yore, unless we count Anne Royall. I envy McGrory's skill in acquiring knowledge about what goes on in the world and admire her for courageously speaking out in no uncertain terms, as she did recently about the massacre in East Timor. In the closing paragraph of her Nov. 20 column, she cited several instances of abuse of human rights and described one of these as "the ultimate, perhaps, in what Western diplomacy has wrought in the Pacific."

I decided to look up definitions and found very interesting descriptions of "sob sister" and "sob story." No mention of obituaries, but a sob story can be described as one which is an "excessively sentimental human interest story," written by a sob sister, who, it seems, might be a *male* journalist. A second-place definition of a sob sister is "a sentimental and ineffective person who seeks to do good." Enough said about that.

I decided to check references for the correct spelling of the name of that very important pioneering newswoman,

Anne Royall. My sources of information about sob sisters did not tell me about this journalist who long ago persistently affected the efforts of statesmen in Washington, so I turned to the writing of Georgia Heaster, whose novel about Royall was serialized in *Hill and Valley* magazine. As I thought of a remark Anne Royall made about our state, Vol. 5, No. 3 of *Hill and Valley* refreshed my memory. *Sketches of History, Life and Manners in the United States by a Traveller* was printed in 1826 for Anne Newport Royall. In it she described the Kanawha Valley very unfavorably, but I am sure, quite accurately because her stage coach or carriage journey took her through this area when hills had been denuded and smoke, possibly from salt processing, filled the air.

I am pleased to announce that copies of the 80 issues of *Hill and Valley* magazine are now in the W. Va. Archives and History Library. Previously, West Virginia University and Brown University were, to my knowledge, the only institutions holding complete sets.

And of course, I know how lucky we are to have cake batter! We hear often about the children who don't have cake. All we have to do is choose whether we will turn away and say, "They should be grateful for a slice of bread."

❧ January 9, 1992 ❧

Many people have seen an older person–perhaps an uncle or a grandparent–peel an apple slowly, carefully, making the peeling paper-thin and attempting (and often succeeding) to produce one long spiral, unbroken. This was considered an accomplishment. I have been thinking of this recently and wondering why succeeding in this manner caused pleasure.

Often in the past apples were plentiful with trees growing in back yards or in orchards and there was no need to make the peeling thin to avoid waste. Besides, the parings were sometimes used to make jelly; it was no great loss if the peeling was not paper-thin. I've concluded that the pleasure was in the doing. If I'm not in too much of a hurry to prepare a meal, I actually enjoy peeling potatoes, taking my time, using a paring knife in preference to slashing away with a potato peeler. However, the shape of a potato doesn't inspire spiral paring and so I realize that an apple has a special quality, and I have no doubt said enough about apples.

*   *   *

Buying postage stamps instead of perfume or a new dress and persistently sending out manuscripts does, indeed, bring welcome results to a writer–sometimes. At last my novel is accepted for publication. No need to tell how many times it has been rejected. One of the "big" editors who sent the manuscript back with a kind letter explained that he isn't sure the book would earn enough money to please me or him. Apparently he doesn't realize how gratifying it can be to have words you have written made available to readers. Although the big name publishers today are accustomed to thinking in terms of millions or billions, according to recent news reports, a scribbler will be pleased if any of his or her words appear in print. I'm grateful to be allowed space for my words about apple peeling, most grateful.

*   *   *

Perhaps it is fitting to spend time during the holidays reading old letters, looking at mementos we have cherished and then discarding some of them. Looking back at the past sometimes helps us appreciate even more people we no longer see. Sometimes we gain better understanding from letters than from face-to-face communication. Realizing this, we can perhaps be more observant and listen more attentively to people who are part of our lives today.

*   *   *

Rereading Helen Hunt Jackson's *Ramona*, written in 1884, I am pleased to find in the opening pages the description of Senora Morena which bolsters my contention concerning women's rights and their accomplishments. I have maintained that throughout the ages women have been more powerful than many people realize. The Senora in this fascinating story "managed everything on the place . . . but nobody, except the Senora knew this."

❧ January 16, 1992 ☙

Receipt of an expensive gadget that is supposed to make life easier for me caused me to think–again–about civilization and my place in it. I've been told a time or two that I should have lived in mid-Victorian days, or in later horse and buggy days, but I doubt if I would be comfortable in either period. I remember that as a child I sat on a sturdy old farm horse for a long time, afraid to have anyone tell it to move. Finally I gave up, reluctantly. I had wanted very much to ride but I couldn't muster enough courage. I doubt if I'd be any braver now and I can't imagine being in charge of horse and buggy. Nor can I picture myself piloting a plane or driving a moving van.

I have a tendency to shy away from push-button tools. I leave them in the box as long as I can get away with it. After a while I may accept and use them, but I'll probably never use all the keys on the typewriter which I bought for myself. I appreciate the typewriter very much, but I have no desire at present to explore the workings of the back trace key or the little arrow on the lower right. I've only had the machine since 1985.

My thinking about modern inventions which are supposedly the result of the progress of civilization leads me to questions. Dining in an air-conditioned room is quite different from dining with someone standing behind your chair to wave a branch or a fan over your head to keep the flies away and cool you a little. Yet, electrical air conditioning has been made possible by the work of men in power plants, some of them working at times in extremely high temperatures, in noise, perhaps in ashes or dust, sometimes crawling through pipes and using welding torches. Consider how steel is produced and how coal is mined. I think of this and then I wonder what comforted or eased the girls who waved the fans over the diners.

It seems that progress quite often creates problems. Making, obtaining and using new products leaves us with the problem of disposal which everyone has heard about today. Author Rudyard Kipling was of the opinion that if men are smart enough to make machines we could manage to control those machines and what the machines produce. The author lived 71 years before his death in 1936 and he may have learned that as early as the thirteenth and fourteenth centuries people were aware of the ill effects of air pollution and he may have known that Edward I had attempted to control it. Mr. Kipling did mention, however, the need for God's aid.

And, speaking of the progress of civilization which often involves changes in customs, I am somewhat curious about the fact that today some men keep their hats on while dining. (No need to mention their failure to remove hats in elevators which was once the custom.) I wonder if keeping their hats on in the presence of women is an indication that they are rebelling against women's requests for equal rights or is it a sign that in this matter, at least, they now consider women their equal?

Today, January 5, 1992, I read a letter written by my brother in 1943. In it he said that he got special leave to go to the railroad station at Charlottesville and that he went through the train looking for me without success. I recall that the train going east was divided at Charlottesville, one section going to Washington and the other to Newport News. Perhaps in haste he boarded the wrong section. Maybe someone gave him the wrong directions. How sorry I am that he didn't find me!

A present-day disappointment: I have learned that it is no longer possible to go by passenger train from Charleston to Newport News, en route to Norfolk. I had hoped to make that trip again someday.

Often, as we recall events, we think chiefly of our own personal experience. We think first of what happened to us at a particular time. Reading letters written by others can give us a jolt, altering our concepts of the past, and perhaps this will help us gain a broader view of what's happening here and now. Coming across a remark like "I came home on No. 8," which referred to traveling on a train from Charleston to East Bank, certainly makes us realize how times have changed since those words were written in the 1940's. And to think of all that has been invented since some of the letters were written is mind-boggling. Imagine your great-grandfather's surprise and confusion if he were able to come back today! However, the changes would be no more unbelievable than the reality facing people whose homes and native cities have been eradicated by the devastation of war or by the building of a super highway.

One of the best results of reading letters from the past: Sometimes we find there was more love and concern among family members than we recall. Occasionally we get a glimmer of light as we are reminded that we sometimes managed to do something nice for another member of the family. I liked reading that cookies I sent were appreciated. I wonder what kind they were.

*   *   *

Watching a highly rated and basically worthwhile movie caused me to think about the means of expressing anger and frustration which were made evident in two ways by a character in the movie–first, by cursing and later, by simply stopping the car he was driving and walking for a few minutes on a deserted desert highway. I thought the latter method was much more likely to evoke the sympathy and understanding of viewers than the first.

We've worn out "cuss words," old and new, by constant overuse. (That we doesn't include me, honestly. I hardly ever feel that angry.) Because of the constant use of "four-letter words" by writers, speakers and people we know, these words have lost their effectiveness. Dealers with words could profit by broadening their skill so that they don't have to resort to the use of ugly-sounding, irrelevant, and sometimes irreverent, words and phrases as they attempt to convey meaning.

❧ January 30, 1992 ❧

I walked down the firm, still-good stairway at the rear of the store, noticed the ceiling-high mirror on the landing and wondered what will happen to it when the store closes. As I walked, I recalled being on those stairs long ago as I looked for my brother who was searching for Christmas gifts. We were shopping without our parents' supervision—a rare occasion. Shopping in Charleston was not an everyday occurrence for us. Shopping anywhere was not an everyday occurrence. We probably had about $2.00 between us, and I tried to tell my brother, four years younger than I, how to spend wisely. He was looking for a gift for our grandmother, and he seemed satisfied after he bought her a large artificial rose and a wash cloth.

Today, January 6, 1992, I bought some wash cloths at the store and a few towels of good quality at a much lower price than I have found elsewhere. I have bought towels here several times, but this will be the last because McCrory's, the last of the Capitol Street "ten cent stores," is closing.

I stood outside the store and looked sadly at the beautiful old buildings, the pleasant street, and I wondered again why the malls were built. I have heard person after person say "I don't like the malls," and some of the people who say this are not as old as I am. I have noticed that opening a shop in the mall is not a guarantee of success. Some spaces have been occupied by several businesses that fail and close. And, everybody knows that mall shopping is harder on your feet than street shopping. Maybe I'll live to see a reversal.

Last week I mentioned anger. Some time ago, I wrote an essay which began with the sentence "Perhaps I have never been angry enough." In this essay, I listed instances when my efforts in behalf of causes had not been strong enough to be effective. Today, I am "angry enough" to mention that I have been thinking of the enormous amounts of money spent on military training as contrasted with the fact that many qualified students today are aware that they may not be able to attend school beyond high school. During World War II, young men who had not attended college previously were sent to topnotch colleges. A naval pilot/navigator was instructed at not one, but three colleges, in addition to training at two large air fields. When the war ended, he was not prepared for any skilled or professional work other than flying. Of course, the G.I. bill provided peacetime training for veterans, but what of the young men and women facing the astronomical cost of higher education today when we are not at war?

I am not "angry enough" to find statistics or conduct interviews so that I might write an impressive article. I am merely "angry enough" to risk being ignored or criticized by readers like those who berated our editor for speaking in a certain way about the use of atomic bombs in World War II.

*   *   *

Once upon a time there were two verbs, *lie* and *lay*. These words were designated for separate usage. Have the rules changed? I thought I knew how to use *sit* and *set*, too, but my application doesn't coincide with that of some of the people on television.

❁ February 6, 1992 ❂

I have heard parents of all ranks, shapes and sizes say they are helping their grown-up sons and daughters pay the rent, or helping pay for the car or the new house—or even helping buy groceries. Information about parents' support usually comes from confidential conversations. Sometimes an admission is made to offer comfort to another parent who has revealed with embarrassment that income received "after the chicks have flown" is still being shared as need arises.

Occasionally we may hear that sons and daughters have been able to repay their parents for the cost of the college education. (This accomplishment is rare, I believe, and is likely to become extinct.) We members of an older generation of parents occasionally look back and recall that cash transactions in the past between parents and their children were often the reverse of what is happening today because in the past young people were often called on to help with their parents' financial needs.

We are somewhat bewildered, at a loss to explain "how things got this way" and as usual, we wonder if we have failed. It may be that we think we have trained our children to manage money wisely. If so, then we may ask if we have been asleep while the economy reached the state it's in. We wonder if we voted for the right people or if we have tried hard enough to understand problems with economy.

Parents often agree that it's not easy to say no when a job is lost, a lawyer is needed, a locale proves unfavorable or someone is ill. Quite often the situation is not so drastic; the young people simply haven't been able to stretch income far enough. However, you can't say, "You've made your bed; now lie in it," when the bed must be left in a furnished apartment because the rent hasn't been paid, or when the furniture is reclaimed because payments are overdue.

Is it perhaps fitting that we can't say no when there is a need? I think what bothers me more than being asked for financial help is becoming aware of problems so great that I volunteer assistance without being asked. Then I do, indeed, wonder if I am doing the wrong thing and so I try to avoid offering help before I am asked. In this way I can go through the motion of treating the assistance not as a gift, but as a sum to be borrowed, put on an account to be repaid when the recipient is able. Thereby, even if I can't say no, I have given the petitioner the dignity of a business-like obligation and have protected myself from thinking that I have been foolishly generous, but it's not easy to sit back and wait for a request, and at times it may be wrong to do so.

Perhaps, after all, it is right that we can't say no. Long ago dowries were furnished, and often several families lived under one roof. Children inherited land. True, sons and daughters were sometimes told they must leave the nest, make their own way, but this is America in the late, late twentieth century. No doubt, parents will continue helping. Perhaps we should be less puzzled and embarrassed because we help.

❧ February 13, 1992 ❧

In a recent column I mentioned reading a 1943 letter. The date I read the letter was January 5, 1992, not 1991–just for the record.

Possibly, the reason I feel tearful when a story has a happy ending: I am sorry for all the people who don't have happy endings. Could it be that I'm sorry for myself because there aren't more fairy-tale solutions in my life and the lives of people close to me? Seems to me I've heard experts say that often when we weep we're being sorry for ourselves. That's a gloomy thought.

All I need to cause me to dismiss for a while thoughts about my comparatively trivial problems is to look at pictures in *National Geographic* or *Time* or to listen to news reports. Maybe it's a good thing that West Virginians were isolated for so long, cut off from the rest of the world, as sociologists say we were. It wasn't so likely that we'd get discouraged and give up as it might have been if we had known more about the deplorable conditions in other parts of the world or if we "hillbillies" had known a little more about facts affecting people in other parts of the United States. Being isolated probably helped build a reservoir of strength, enabling us to cope more easily when "freed" from isolation.

Today our conceptions about people and their needs, problems of space (earth space, not extraterrestrial) and the importance of time can be altered by considering seriously statistics such as the number of men trained in WW II, the amount of planning needed and the huge transportation problem involved when our entire country was deeply involved in war. After reading a few letters from servicemen, which so often included mention of food, we "ordinary citizens," never having been called on to work with enormous numbers of people, can get an inkling concerning the amount of effort involved in feeding so many–this in addition to the task of clothing and equipping them.

I have just finished reading *Saying Goodbye* by M. R. Montgomery, which gives an insight into the construction problems of the WW II era, with bases sometimes planned, begun and left unfinished, but with a huge amount of construction accomplished. This book, published by Knopf in 1989, also gives me a glimpse of the barren stretches of land in Montana and connects my thought with the letter of a West Virginia serviceman stationed in Texas who said he hadn't seen a "real tree" in such a long time. (It's good that we still have trees and that some effort to protect them has been made.)

This scribbling, having created a hodgepodge of thought, has led me to thinking of Pollyanna. What's wrong with being a Pollyanna, anyway? As I recall, that young lady didn't just go around saying everyone should be glad; she did a few practical things to help others find happiness. If she were here today, she might say that I should be glad that some of the planning going on in our country now is not concerned with war efforts. Problems other than the need for fighting are being considered; some of these plans may be of benefit to citizens who are not being prepared to go to war.

    ❂ February 20, 1992 ✎

Many people may recall hearing someone, possibly a grandmother, say rather sternly, "Beauty is as beauty does." That's a good saying, but it hasn't been prominent in my mind since I decided a long time ago that the way I look need not have much bearing on my survival. Another quotation about beauty has been of interest to me in recent years–"Beauty is in the eyes of the beholder." (Does that remind you of the saying about the woman who kissed the cow? That's beside the point and my scribbling is rambling, so back to beauty and the beholder.) Surely I didn't make up or invent that saying. I couldn't find it in Bartlett's quotations this morning, but I like it and have a few related statements to make.

Once upon a time, when I was in no position to furnish a home of my own, I saw a display of furniture that seemed to be exactly the kind of dream furniture I would like–color scheme and all. Need I say that it is a far cry from furniture we've had and been glad to have in our home since that day? If we had bought that special furniture, which I think was in Woodrums' window, it would probably have been worn out by now. At least, the beautiful pastel upholstery would have been repaired or replaced.

I remember that window display, but I have put the recollection aside without pain. An important discovery has helped make adjustment easy. Looking at a photograph taken in our house made me aware of a noteworthy fact in reference to our home and its decoration or lack of decoration: How I look at what I see is important.

Members of the family are in the photograph taken near the hutch cabinet in our dining room. The cabinet is not "store bought." It was made from an old, old dresser I inherited from my mother, one of two which she acquired when we moved into a house that may have been a coal camp boarding house. Two sturdy oak dressers had been left in the house by former tenants. My husband made an open dish cabinet using one of the dressers as a base. The cabinet is rather handsome and very useful, and I am pleased to have it. However, many times during busy days I have glanced at the cabinet filled with dishes and glassware and thought, "It's too cluttered; it looks messy," or "It needs straightening," or "It's dusty."

The photograph gave me an entirely different picture. The cabinet and its odd assortment of dining ware look interesting, attractive and even glamorous in the picture. As I thought of this and looked at other photos made in our house, I gave considerable thought to the fact that the way I look at things make a difference.

I have often smugly told myself, my children and anyone else who cared to listen that I consider many things more important than expensive furniture and carpets. I do, but in the busy everyday world I was sometimes dissatisfied with what I saw. The photo reminded me that I can enjoy sunlight coming through a window even if the window isn't sparkling clean, but I really should dust the dish cabinet and its contents more often. Perhaps I will. Incidentally, did the old woman kiss a cow or a pig? It's possible that my mind clutter needs straightening, too.

🌿 February 27, 1992 🌿

Criticism (kinds of, need for, need to avoid) is a subject I should perhaps devote little space to, but since I read a chapter of a book by Amy Tan yesterday afternoon and came across a related thought in an old notebook, my mind has been filled with thoughts about criticism, which is definitely a problem for many of us, either as we offer criticism or as we are the object of criticism. I doubt if there are many adults who haven't chafed under criticism at one time or another.

The notebook I was looking at yesterday has entries made in 1941, including my observation that criticism is a disease "to which the best of us seem susceptible" and I mentioned that I had been experiencing a year-long attempt to adjust to unexpected resentment and criticism. I remember thinking when I was younger (before 1941) that my mother never praised anything I did except when she was talking to other people about me. That, of course, is rather a childish thought; we usually know without being told when our parents are proud of our accomplishments. I think what we don't like is being told we should have done something differently, because a certain method would be better.

However , having been a mother for a long time now, I find it is difficult, if not impossible, to refrain from saying (occasionally, of course), "Perhaps you should have done so and so," or "I always put the milk in first," or some such. As a result, I, like other mothers, have heard, at least once, "You never think I do anything right."

I found very interesting Amy Tan's portrayal in *The Kitchen God's Wife* of the mother-daughter relationship. When the daughter and her husband and children go to her mother's house for a brief visit, they are somewhat annoyed when the mother keeps asking if everything is all right in the guest room, if the heat needs turned up, if they have enough towels, etc., etc. And I thought, "That's something I would probably do." If we have visitors, I want to be sure they have what they need. (So???) This relates to children's criticism of parents, and it serves to illustrate that family relations even in the best of circumstances can be difficult.

In Tan's novel the daughter doesn't want the mother to know that she has multiple sclerosis because she wants to escape from constant discussions, questions or even blame. This is understandable if we recall how often a parent said, "How did you get that cold?" and if we think about how the question made us feel.

A recent news article describing a satisfactory adjustment made when a married couple moved into an elderly parent's home mentioned that it is rather difficult to get used to–again–being told to put on a sweater when you go out. It seems to me that I may fit quite snugly into the unwanted reminder category, but mothers have always known when it's sweater weather.

Scribbling at length has produced no solution to problems related to criticism; perhaps adding to awareness is enough. I really should avoid know-it-all statements on this subject. Sometimes some of our children read my column. One of our sons hinted that he couldn't quite endorse my "scientific" statement about wires, the windmill and a generator. (Remember?) Criticism is contagious; sometimes it helps. Doesn't it?

❧ March 5, 1992 ☙

We have so much–Perhaps it's just as well that we don't often stop to think about what we take for granted. I push a button and the conversation ends, the voice is gone. There isn't even a wire connecting me directly in a tangible way. I am holding a cordless phone. My aunt, miles away, many miles–I would have to travel through several states to see her–tells me what she's preparing to cook for her evening meal; she tells me of the success of her birthday celebration with her three sons together again. I hear the familiar voice, imagine how she looks, then pressing a button ends the contact which was initiated by pressing buttons. I really don't want to go back to horse and buggy days; some things we have are very valuable. It would be wonderful if we could eliminate some of the things that cause hurt and destruction and keep only the good.

Why did I say it may be just as well that we don't stop to think about inventions we take for granted? Perhaps because the wonder would be mind-boggling. Perhaps if we think about how remarkable some of our present-day conveniences are, we might begin to fear the possibility of materialization of some of the gruesome events pictured in late-night movies, such as self-operating machines which destroy people. I'm glad I feel inclined to see a late-late movie only about once a year. My mind might really become boggled if I watched more.

A letter written several years ago—actually I should say *many* years ago, as measured by the majority of people who live today. (I wonder what the word *several* means, exactly.) Perhaps I should say a great many years ago, since 49 or 50 years is a great number to many people living today. Okay, to make it simpler: A letter written approximately 50 years ago mentions discovery of a gastronomical delight, a food prepared in a way unfamiliar to the writer—french-fried sweet potatoes. I've never eaten sweet potatoes prepared in that way, and I've never seen them on a menu anywhere. I wonder what is included in the preparation.

The first definition of *several* that I find tells me that 50 years is probably, or undoubtedly, more than several because several means more than two but less than many. Yet I suppose the meaning is flexible depending on who's counting.

       *   *   *

There is a difference between submission and acceptance, and a quotation familiar to many mentions the need for wisdom when deciding whether or not one should try to change things. West Virginians, I think, and my opinion is contrary to the opinion of those who accuse us of being too passive, have demonstrated their wisdom in this matter. I recall having heard, at times, "There's no use butting your head against a brick wall," and that seems rather sensible to me, in spite of the fact that I've never given up mentioning occasionally that I think war is horrible and uncivilized.

A related subject: Humility, a good quality at times. Hobert Skidmore included humility in his list of qualities admirable in West Virginians. In one of his *Saturday Evening Post* stories a young soldier says West Virginians are friendly, but not pushy like people in other places.

❧ March 12, 1992 ❧

Perhaps our progress in some respects isn't as rapid or as remarkable as we think, proportionately. I have just learned that the ancient Inca people developed a method of freeze-drying potatoes so that they could be easily stored and saved for times when crops were scarce. According to the February issue of *National Geographic*, the method they used consisted of letting the potatoes freeze during the night, then pressing the water out the next day, with the result a light-weight, easily preserved food. After European conquerors took charge of Inca affairs, preservation of food was neglected and the beautifully terraced gardens were not put to the best use. Sometimes it seems that instead of going two steps forward and one back, we reverse the procedure. Now, about four hundred and fifty years after the Incas flourished, we can buy packages of "preserved" ready-to-cook potatoes at the grocery store.

For a while I thought I had nothing else to say just now–no scribbling to add to the one paragraph I jotted down a day or two ago–not this week, even though I have something to be very glad about. A few days ago I was very fearful and almost certain that a serious accident had harmed a family member. Due to a misunderstanding, perhaps my fault, I spent a miserable hour under unusual circumstances, waiting for someone who didn't come. I was, of course, relieved to find that person was safe, but the event seems to have left me wordless, almost.

As always, I am nearly overwhelmed by knowledge of all the harm and hurt that go on in the world. Since my husband and I are both retired, even from volunteer work, at present, we both spend quite a bit of time reading the morning paper immediately after breakfast, except on days when he goes fishing. (Even then, he looks at the paper briefly before he leaves.) Today the item that really left me speechless for the moment was news that two students died after being shot in the hallway of a Brooklyn high school.

What can I find good about today's news? The fact that we have newspapers is good, I think. The fact that people are free to talk and argue is good. Students are reading, I see. High school students are registering to vote. The fact that people of two communities have been told to boil water is good. We can be glad that civilization has progressed to the point of establishing an agency to monitor water conditions.

It's hard to believe that two of five people in West Virginia can't read street signs or the names of buses, but having our attention called to the statistic may help lead to a remedy. We can hope.

Having a little space left, and thinking I might find another "thought" to add to these words, I picked up a four page paper someone sent me thinking it might interest me because it deals with the subject of catastrophes and attempts to provide an answer to people who ask why disasters occur. The first phrase that held my attention was "words without knowledge." It is good that we have newspapers, isn't it, inasmuch as they can add to our knowledge?

ae March 26, 1992 he

Thought provoking words in a *Time* Magazine article about the shooting of two youths in a Brooklyn school: " . . . a world that has given the young neither self-discipline nor much to hope for." Helping young people develop self-discipline is difficult and I, for one, cannot make a list and say, "If you follow these guidelines you can be certain that self-discipline will become a reality governing your children." Surely, however, we adults can try to avoid being overwhelmed by conditions in the world and manage somehow to demonstrate to young people "that work may sometimes help us" advance toward goals that will make life better, eliminating injustice and cruelty, for example.

*   *   *

Preparing to speak to and talk with a junior college class studying Appalachian literature, I plan to ask the students if and why they think Appalachian literature is worth preserving. Doing so, I most definitely will mention–again–the Skidmore twins whose writing has been acclaimed by authorities in high posts. Both Hubert and Hobert have written books published by leading firms and Hobert's writing has been reprinted in many countries, but the work of these West Virginia natives has not received the attention it deserves in their home state. A letter from Hobert told me not to worry about this, but I do, and I still hope that their writings can be preserved.

*   *   *

As I looked from the front door of our "city" home, observing signs of spring, I thought of looking out the front door of our coal community home on Cabin Creek long ago. We lived very close to the railroad and a sidetrack which held loaded coal cars brought down from the coal tipple to wait for the train which would take them away. Early in the morning this sidetrack would be clear. The appearance of the cars was not distracting; we hardly noticed the screech and thump that announced each arrival. Of course, once a car "got away" and overturned, spilling coal not far from our house, but no one was hurt. Across the track were a neighbor's house and a building converted from a blacksmith shop to a place for holding church services. Next, a road for cars, the creek and the hill. We enjoyed the coming of spring in that coal camp setting. Life was not desolate, except occasionally, as it is everywhere. Luckily, we were not hungry; we were not rebellious; we were not bemoaning our fate. We could look up at the sky and the hills. I enjoyed sitting on our clean, often scrubbed porch, reading.

In the beginning of a book about West Virginia coal mining people Jack Weller's list of questions includes these: Why do people sit on their porches? Are they lazy? Near the end of the book he says that he and his wife have learned that they, too, can find time to sit in a swing and enjoy the beauty of mountains. As I look at our front yard (in the city) I see a persistent crocus, product of bulbs my mother planted long ago when she visited us here. The primrose from my mother-in-law's Kentucky lawn is blooming, and the rose bushes my husband cares for are alive and well. I have a "carry-over" from our coal camp life. We open our doors in the summer and we open drapes to let in the light, year-round, and here, too, I can watch the trains go by.

Too late, I realized that I should have written community college instead of junior college in last week's column. The envelope had been sealed and placed in the mail box. Often we think more clearly after the opportunity to speak is past. Hindsight is better than foresight? Then it follows that studying the past is important and hindsight and foresight can blend, perhaps proving the strength of the statement that he is not a fool who makes a mistake once, but who makes the same mistake twice. Being a forgiving soul, always hoping for a better world, I will modify that statement: It is to be expected that some mistakes will be made twice. If I leave out the baking powder for a cake twice, I don't feel that I'm a fool; I just realize that I have to try harder to be less absent-minded. I need to concentrate more on the recipe and less on what I said, or didn't say, or will say while scribbling, and I need to think about what happens to a cake made without baking powder. So be it, I hope.

*   *   *

We sometimes complain that TV stations don't keep the "good programs, the ones we really like, those that are worthy and well-done," but we fail to make our preferences known. I've been putting off for days writing to NBC. I want to thank them for bringing back "I'll Fly Away."

*   *   *

In a 1988 issue of *Triquarterly* I found a section of poems from Poland. I was struck by a line about adolescents who "long for forgiveness for having lived timidly," and I wonder how many of us have lived too timidly. How should we speak? Elections are coming. How should we vote? We can be glad (There I go again!) that young people whose letters have appeared in the new Expressions section of *The Charleston Gazette* have not been too timid to speak out, and that some of them earn their spending money and some even save money. One admitted being spoiled.

*   *   *

A writer whose name I have forgotten stated in an article that only a fanatic tells the truth all the time. He implied that it is often courteous to fail to tell the truth. An example might be that when invited to go somewhere you don't want to go, you may politely supply a reason for not going which isn't truthful. It seems to me that only harm can come from lying. If someone asks me, "Do you like my dress?" and I reply, "I like the color," should I also add, "I like some of your other dresses better?" I think I should. The questioner may want an honest opinion. In the closing pages of Pearl Buck's novel, *The Rainbow*, a character is said to have "long ago" discovered lying to be a refuge of the weak. I was impressed by this statement, and then I remembered that the character had told a business associate to go ahead and start a rival company, seeming to give his blessing, and then immediately set out to undermine and destroy that person's venture. Perhaps he learned about lying after that "incident." Is it possible that he thought, "It's different in the business world?"

◁ April 9, 1992 ▷

Why do children fail to close doors? Surely their leaving doors ajar or even wide open at times could become a subject for analysis. Perhaps an important research paper might grow from the question. Possibly this could be a subject for government research. I don't want the assignment. Although I am definitely not a child, I sometimes leave doors and drawers open, and a few times, to my sorrow, have seen an adult who happens to be taller than I, get a nasty bang on the head because I've left open a kitchen cabinet door, but I'm getting better about this.

First off, a researcher might want to investigate the possibility that discipline is not what it used to be in the days when an irritated adult might ask, "What's the matter? Were you raised in a barn?" However, I wouldn't pursue this angle. My mother was a very strict disciplinarian, and I dreaded very much and tried hard to avoid getting a lecture for leaving the closet door in my room only slightly ajar, and the results of her efforts aren't perfect, as I have pointed out.

That reminds me: I am happy to see that Dr. Benjamin Spock, pediatrician, is alive and energetically defending his position on the care of children, refusing to accept blame for all the rebellion of the Vietnam era. Dr. Spock's book on baby and child care was first published at a time when parents were glad to be told that it was all right to show affection for their children and that it wasn't necessary to force oneself to stand by and listen in anguish as a baby cried. Previously, child care experts had said strict schedules must be kept, no matter what. The book is now in its sixth printing and the 88-year-old doctor, who has a pacemaker and is on a diet, is receiving handsome royalties from his book which was first published in 1946 and has sold 40 million copies. The doctor was involved in opposition to our entry in the Vietnam war, but insists that he advised firm guidance of children. I recall particularly his helpful advice about foods and his emphasizing that parents should use common sense in treating their children as individuals whose needs might vary.

I have been surprised recently by discovering that honor students, college graduates, and others sometimes know little or nothing about any war before the last one, or the two latest. This should not come as such a great surprise, however, since many of us recall that in history classes we never seemed to get through all the wars. This lack of knowledge may explain the fact that the general public is accustomed to letting the president, the ambassadors, the diplomats, and sometimes congressmen, make all the decisions that determine whether or not we'll have another war. We go calmly about our daily life, unaware of impending possibilities. We fail to vote and seldom or never write to our representatives in Washington. Probably, we never think of such a thing as "asking for forgiveness for having lived timidly."

*   *   *

I see that Chris Miller, writing for the *Charleston Sunday Gazette Mail*, is not pleased with all of Phyllis Naylor's award-winning book for children, set in West Virginia. The reviewer tells us that a very unfavorable impression of life in our state is presented. This happens too often, in my opinion.

◬ April 16, 1992 ◭

At this point in time–Whom am I quoting, and why didn't that person just say now?–At this point in time, I am getting a little bit tired of my perfectionist tendencies. I am not quite so eager to go back to check to be sure I turned the light off or wiped up the thimbleful of water I spilled, thinking that if I failed to dry up the water, someone might fall. No doubt about it, I have aged considerably since I wrote a story about a death caused when someone didn't go back to check a locked door. That story was published three times. Only one appearance was in my own magazine, so it must have appealed to the other two editors who chose to publish it, one in West Virginia and one in Kentucky.

It seems that often accidents are caused by carelessness and disregard, but many of my perfectionist activities have to do with what some would term nit-picking. If I have tried to teach children that they must always do thus and so, I feel compelled to always do thus and so myself. (It is possible that I forget sometimes or fail as a monitor. Washing fingerprints from kitchen cabinets while I wait for brownies to bake, I decided I must keep trying to observe the rules.) A doctor told me once that it would drive anyone crazy to try to keep a house in a sanitary condition. People who have been in our house within the last ten or fifteen years will probably feel like laughing aloud when they read this. I haven't even kept a very clean house for a long time, but I still go around nit-picking. However, when we're leaving home these days, most of the time members of my family don't feel compelled to drive around the block and let me go into the house again to see if everything is as it should be. Perhaps that's progress. Often I can lock the door and promptly walk away.

Artists and writers may be hampered and their creations may lack style or appeal if they insist on perfection in work they produce. And yet, strict realism and accuracy have merit.

*   *   *

If I try to explain to a class or to people attending a workshop why writers write or why I write, it occurs to me that a factor may be a combination of conceit and a sense of inferiority. We want to be heard. We may feel that talking is not the solution. If we put words on paper, we aren't likely to be present when someone reads those words. We can tell ourselves that surely someone will read them, perhaps be impressed, and we can glow with satisfaction if we learn that someone did read them.

*   *   *

I have now read more than half of Joyce Carol Oates' *Because It Is Bitter and Because It Is My Heart.* I put the book aside soon after I bought it because a very unfortunate, unsavory, disabled creature was identified as having come from West Virginia to live in Hammond, New York. Yesterday. I read that the "poor soul" was much happier because she had gone back to West Virginia. In the intervening pages, a member of the migratory family was murdered; he had been portrayed as being so obnoxious that readers were not likely to bemoan his death. Why do writers do this? The place name West Virginia must have some special attraction for out-of-state writers. We must try harder to promote writing about West Virginians that presents positive pictures.

❧ April 23, 1992 ☙

In the past when I heard the words "Pulitzer Prize," vague thoughts about the glory of winning a prestigious award for writing might flash through my mind and be dismissed quickly so that I could concentrate on goals close at hand. I might think briefly on the fact that it's very nice of someone to establish such awards. Until I saw a movie this past weekend, I had no idea that Joseph Pulitzer might be considered as a villain hungry for power and willing to disregard the hardships of the newsboys who delivered his papers on the streets of New York in the 1890's. The movie was "Newsies," and the newsboys went on strike because Mr. Pulitzer ordered an increase in the price the boys paid when they bought newspapers to peddle, making the youngsters' profits less and Pulitzer's profits greater, according to the film.

I found no reference to such villainy in my quick search of references, but we aren't always told all the facts in all the books. In the motion picture, the "happy ending" came when youthful employees of other businesses joined the newsboys' protest. After mentioning child labor laws to my granddaughter, I checked and found that it was not until 1938 that firm child labor controls became law in the United States.

Another fact learned belatedly: Today's morning newspaper tells me that the American Indians forced to leave their homes in 1838 to follow the "Trail of Tears" left well-established homes and communities where they had become part of the European settlers' culture. I found this fact in a review of a book by Jerry Ellis, a Cherokee descendant who recently walked the 900-mile trail.

Again considering facts, what should we think about some of the things we're hearing about poll taking? This seems especially important at election time.

A friend helping me edit a manuscript questioned the fictional "fact" that people in a coal community could live very near each other without seeing each other for days at a time. I checked with my husband to be sure about the reality of coal camp life as we knew it. He often went to work before daylight, leaving his home about 4:00 or 4:30 a.m. This meant that women would probably be up at that hour, fixing breakfast and lunches for the men. By the time the long work-day ended, the miners and women in their households would be very tired. There was no constant visiting back and forth in the coal communities. You could live next door to someone for years and never go inside that neighbor's house. That's one reason going to the company store was so important. You could see people there you would never see elsewhere. My husband used to tease me by saying that somehow I managed to be cutting the hedge in front of our house just at the time when he might be coming home from work. Maybe I should remind him that there was more than one way to come down the hill from the mine. He didn't have to choose the path that came down the hill behind our house.

*   *   *

Words worth repeating: "War is a last-resort solution . . . [which] should not rest on a president's whim or political agenda." These words appeared March 31, in a *Charleston Gazette* editorial.

⚛ April 30, 1992 ⚛

It is difficult to learn the whole truth about what's happening today, and, although in some respects it is easier to learn the truth about the past, it is almost impossible, it seems, to be sure we have enough access to facts. Still interested in finding facts about Joseph Pulitzer, after seeing the musical *Newsies*, I hurriedly chose two library books. One was catalogued as biography; the other as a book for young adults. Although I have found much of interest and have enjoyed both books, I found no evidence to support the motion picture portrayal of Pulitzer as a heartless publisher who raised the price the newsboys had to pay for the papers they sold. Both books emphasized Pulitzer's concern for the working man, and the book by W.J. Granberg states that Pulitzer described a great newspaper as one which never lacks sympathy for the poor. I did find, however, that, according to Iris Noble's book, Bennett of the *New York Herald* cut the profit news dealers handling his papers were getting from one half to one third of a cent a copy. Although there was always rivalry among the newspapers, I found no statement attributing such an action to Pulitzer.

I did find a contradiction that seems important. One of the books says that a young man working with Pulitzer drowned while they were traveling. The other book says that he did not drown, but saved himself by holding to the branches of a tree. Regrettably, one page has been torn from Noble's book. Why do people let such damage happen to a book?

Iris Noble's book about Pulitzer was published in 1957. I find it especially interesting that she quotes Joseph Pulitzer as having said, in 1883, "Unfortunately, the Democrats aren't convinced they can win. They aren't thinking big enough. They aren't looking for the kind of man . . . who could win."

*　　　　　　　*　　　　　　　*

I also find it interesting that, in 1992, a detergent manufacturing company boasts of its biodegradable product and boxes made of recycled paper, but provides, without our asking, mountains of plastic scoops which we don't need, a new one in each box.

*　　　　　　　*　　　　　　　*

I'm quite willing to admit that there are things I don't understand. Style, fashion, modes of dress–these are things I don't understand. What is the reasoning or the psychology which influences the wearing apparel of men and women, especially in the United States? A visitor to an office is announced, and the man who is being visited puts on his coat before the visitor enters. He must be properly dressed in his business suit, wearing a tie. Yet a woman visitor may be wearing an outfit suitable for the beach or a garden party. The differences in formal evening clothes are especially puzzling. A man is completely clad, bound by stiffness, cuff links, a cummerbund, even. A woman may be wearing almost nothing. Hats for women are coming back, and sometimes women wear gloves, but in contrast, skirts are shorter, almost disappearing. What is the explanation?

*   *   *

Joseph Pulitzer by Iris Noble, Julian Messner, Inc.

The World of Joseph Pulitzer by W.J. Granberg, Abelard-Schuman.

◁ May 7, 1992 ▷

During the weekend following the California earthquake my husband and I were in Kentucky attending a gathering of poets, pleasant, friendly people interested in writing. (A fishing lake is on the property where the meeting is held.) The wood carving and whittling products my husband took along received more applause than my poems, but I don't mind. He works harder at his craft. I don't consider myself a poet, although a few of my collections of words shaped like poems have been published, some even paid for. I write because I want to, and have been told that I write poems sometimes because I want to make a statement, and in some circles, that is a no-no for poetry. However, these words came to mind after we returned home and listened to a news report:

TOO MUCH OF WHAT?

In Kentucky on the side road
A cow sits sad in the mud,
Sad and sick while lush green fields
Lie plentiful beyond the fence,

65

But the creature is bound.

In California a brick house crumbles
And an elderly woman calmly says,
"No, I'm not angry.
Aren't we supposed to accept?"
In China, more than fifty years ago,
As the bombs fell, someone said,
"There are too many of us, anyway."

A book published in 1936, used as a college text, quotes Horace Gregory as saying, while discussing the work of an American poet, that the poet's creations are "manifestations of a civilization that seems childishly innocent and harmlessly insane." * I doubt that we Americans are as naive as we were in 1936, and perhaps we can no longer be described as "harmlessly insane." However, such a possibility might be an appropriate subject for study.

Mentioning insanity reminds me of a statement I read several years ago concerning people who are considered insane and have been placed in asylums, and children, who are usually considered sane and are still in nurseries. I have wondered exactly what the saying means. Perhaps it is one of those "imponderables" that will always leave us wondering. The sentence went something like this: Only in asylums and nurseries do men hear the angels sing. Does this mean that we must think as children do in order to learn the truth? Or does it mean something quite different?

*   *   *

I have always wondered why the small, wild strawberries that grow around our lawns and gardens are not eaten by birds. What is the reason?

Modern American Poetry and Modern British Poetry, Harcourt, Brace and Co.

❧ May 14, 1992 ❧

When our five children were young they wore hand-me-down clothing sometimes, and clothes I made for them, sometimes. Occasionally each child had something bought especially for him or her. (I remember one time when the something new from the mail order company didn't fit well, even after being altered, but the wearer survived and by the time he reached "prom" age was rather handsome and popular among his peers.) Photographs taken years ago show our sons and daughters wearing clothes that are presentable, even though we can identify some of the outfits as "second-hand."

In recent years I have found it hard to understand why, with this background, when these young people first earn money, they often buy far more clothes than they need, beautiful clothes, sometimes more than they can afford, and then, after a while they leave the handsome clothes hanging and wear shabby jeans and sweat shirts. The beautiful clothes hang neglected and I feel somewhat ashamed–not because they are wearing jeans, but because they have bought so many clothes that are not being worn. However, I do appreciate the fact that they are no longer being extravagant. I also appreciate the fact that they sometimes buy pretty clothes as gifts for me.

*   *   *

Members of the fraternal organization, a lodge, support worthy humanitarian projects, but a parade I saw on the first Saturday in May puzzles me. There is quite a diversity, a contrast between the worthy aims and the impression created by a scimitar-wielding person dressed in

67

Oriental costume, and I have mixed thoughts about seeing the line of young men not in costume walking along holding a heavy rope. They were part of the parade and I suppose are being initiated.

Throughout the years many organizations have had initiation ceremonies, and some of their rites have been banned. I attended Marshall before it became M.U., so long ago that we first-year women staying in College Hall were initiated, but the experience was painless and rather enjoyable. I recall only having to crawl through a tire suspended from the ceiling in the dark and dusty basement, and listening to an upper class woman recite a funny story. That experience was quite different from rites of adulthood we learn about which seem frightening to contemplate as they occur in other countries. It is a little bit cruel, of course, to send or take a newcomer to an Appalachian community snipe hunting, directing him to hunt on a mountain, but I've never heard that anyone was harmed greatly by the process.

       *   *   *

Speaking of clothes, I don't understand why people tolerate and consider stylish garments decorated with an insignia, a name, or a miniature creature which advertises another product. The high price on such a piece of clothing pays for customer-financed advertising. Of course, we pay for advertising all the time, but wearing an expensive shirt that advertises a brand of shoes seems too cooperative.

◁ May 21, 1992 ▷

A letter from my uncle, written in 1965, includes this sentence: "To me it is mystery, alive, boundless, and dangerous." He was writing about the sea. Speculating about the impression our children would retain after having seen an ocean for the first time, he wrote, " . . . they saw a little of the anger of the sea as the whitecaps rolled at our feet. I doubt their minds being able to picture the scenes as reality–it will seem more like a dream or a picture–a vast, restless seething sea."

This uncle of mine, Jack Stover, grew up on a West Virginia farm at Colcord. He left the farm, served in the army in World War I, received degrees from Davis and Elkins and the University of Kentucky, and spent many happy years, teaching, coaching and directing community recreation in his native state. After retiring, he and his wife moved to Florida, where he found retirement chafing and soon found work to do tutoring and giving private instruction. (He urged me to give my mother tasks to do when she came to live with us, saying that retirement is "for the birds.")

I think he found the ocean both mystifying and fascinating, feeling perhaps that gazing at the ocean gives one a sense of trying to see into infinity or understand eternity. In the sentence I have quoted he speaks of the mystery and danger of the sea. Perhaps he was somewhat frightened at times. Most of us experience fear or dread occasionally, but his demeanor, product of his strength of character, was such that he remained calm, strong, sedate and dignified, providing a good example for us to follow, even as we are confronted by the vast sea of problems and dangers we face in 1992.

*   *   *

Television cameras show us a woman carrying toilet paper from a demolished store, and we realize that most of us don't know how difficult it is for some families to buy toilet tissue or soap, or to pay the water bill on time.

*   *   *

69

Perhaps there is a small benefit to be gained from reading statements offered in a form that could be called poetry. Five lines, carefully considered and formulated, can say what an essayist or a columnist might require five full paragraphs to say.

*   *   *

The annual conference of West Virginia Writers, Inc. will be held June 5, 6, and 7 at Cedar Lakes Conference Center near Ripley. Workshops will be offered in prose, poetry, religious writing, writing for children, writing for young adults, songwriting and drama. Beginning writers and experienced writers may expect to benefit from attending. For information contact President Pat Love, P.O. Box 5205, Charleston, W.V. 25361.

❧ May 28, 1992 ☙

Spending two days at a delightful vacation place which provides a reading room filled with books and comfortable chairs enabled me to make a discovery. On a shelf holding books that were important to the person chiefly responsible for the development and present-day condition of the establishment, I found several volumes of Sandburg's biography of Abraham Lincoln. Delving into one of the volumes, reading sections here and there, made me fully aware of the fact that Abraham Lincoln was real, alive, and warmly human.

I am convinced that additional reading of this very skillfully written biography would be worthwhile and entertaining. I found the personal letters fascinating.

Incidentally, I've learned that Carl Sandburg won a Pulitzer prize for the last of the six volumes of his biography of Lincoln. This work has been described as exalting

Lincoln as the "symbol and embodiment of the American spirit."

Editors of *The Atlantic* are currently remembering Lincoln. Their June issue features Lincoln on the magazine cover and an article describes his Gettysburg Speech as "words that remade America." The editors seem to be wishing that we may somehow find leaders for our country who will have "even a small fraction" of wisdom and leadership ability such as Lincoln had.

And that reminds me: People I have talked with, young and old, say they have felt a reluctance to go to the polls to vote this year such as they have never before experienced. They voted, they say, but have not done so happily.

*   *   *

Why shouldn't a coal company or lumber company currently operating a profitable business pay taxes based on the current value of their property?

*   *   *

Something else I've learned this week: Carl Sandburg wrote a novel titled *Remembrance Rock*. I'd like to see a copy. Perhaps I can find one. Previously I've always thought of him simply as being the author of the poem about the fog creeping on cat feet and some other poems that I enjoyed. I recall that his daughter made a speech at a luncheon meeting at the Daniel Boone Hotel (in Charleston) once. I was there, I think, but I don't remember what she said.

❧ June 4, 1992 ❧

I paused near a television set, looked at the screen for a minute, just long enough to see a car, or what was left of it, shoot straight up into the air. What could I say or write about that? I thought of the happy, gleeful, holiday crowd joyfully watching the races. I reminded myself: If you aren't sure what you should say, you shouldn't say it.

*   *   *

In the small community where I grew up nearly everyone, it seemed, went to every funeral service. I don't know how many people attended because I was never allowed to attend. It seems that when I was very young, three or four years of age, living in another community, my mother took me to a funeral service held in the home of neighbors who lived across the lane from our house. Perhaps I was affected by this experience in a way my mother thought unfortunate. She never explained why she didn't want me to go to funeral services.

When I was in junior high school, a young man visiting a family who lived near us was killed in an automobile accident. I had seen him only once, but I had met him at a party, and I found it hard to accept the reality of this sudden, unexpected death. I did not attend his funeral. I wrote a letter to my English teacher about this happening and my confusion. Since she was an understanding, helpful teacher she answered my letter.

I recall, too, seeing a motion picture that portrayed a suicide. This was disturbing. Today it is doubtful that anyone grows up without knowledge of the reality of death. We are confronted constantly with portrayals of death in all its forms. Television, magazines and newspapers show us death in wars, in famines, in murderous attacks, even in stories meant to entertain. However, young people today are shocked by death near at hand and often are not prepared to make an adjustment. Counseling is needed and it is good that help is provided.

It is frightening to consider the effect on very young children in situations where they may see vast numbers of people die around them. Such losses have occurred in the past when entire villages might be wiped out by plagues or disease or by raiders. Today destruction continues.

*　　　　　*　　　　　*

Privileged to read and critique plays written by high school students, I was somewhat surprised to find very few plays with happy endings. Many were concerned with death. The eighteen plays I read, written by students in widely scattered locations in the state, dealt with ten deaths. Six of the deaths dramatized were suicidal. Two were the result of murder. I have been told that young people, even in the best of times, are often more likely to write about death than they are to write about love, even though love is very important to them. Yet, I was somewhat overwhelmed by the trend of the plays. I must try to remain hopeful and remind myself that Shakespeare gave them an example, combining love and death, when he wrote of Romeo and Juliet.

❧ June 11, 1992 ☙

An article in the June 8 issue of *Time* magazine reports that only 9,000 of the 36,000 Haitians stopped at sea have been given the right to seek asylum. President Bush has said that we will welcome people who are politically oppressed but that he will not "open the doors to economic refugees." Many people, Cathy Booth's article states, do not want our country to accept more refugees at this time.

After I looked at the issue of *Time*, I picked up, purely by chance, a 1984 issue of *The Atlantic* and found in

73

it a letter from a representative of the United Nations Commission for Refugees. The letter spoke of the need to be sure that refugees wanted to return home.

However, Al Santoli, in a reply to that letter, stated that in 1983 the U.N. Office of the Commissioner for Refugees had suggested that the holding camps should provide an atmosphere so unfavorable that refugees would request return to "the place of persecution from which they had fled." This was in the July, 1984 issue of *The Atlantic*, page 8.

*   *   *

My husband and I enjoyed a weekend in Ohio which included a graduation party for our granddaughter, a high school graduate. This is the second time we have attended such a festivity in Ohio. It seems that Ohioans look at high school graduation as a sort of coming-of-age time when parents, grandparents, and friends, young and old, enjoy getting together to celebrate.

*   *   *

Wallace Stegner, one of my favorite authors, devotes considerable space in his latest book to descriptions of the western section of the United States. He loves the West, but wants to impress readers with the fact that it is arid and colorful but without vast stretches of green. This is definitely a contrast to what we see as we travel the highways in our area this year where we see green, green and more green everywhere. Probably we do not fully appreciate it. I heard someone say, "Traveling on the interstate is rather boring." I must admit it is a little more entertaining to explore side roads, but we find vast stretches of green there, too.

The book I am reading is non-fiction, titled *Where the Bluebird Sings to the Lemonade Springs*, published by

Random House. In the past I have enjoyed Stegner's fiction, especially *The Spectator Bird* and *Crossing to Safety*. The latter deals beautifully with facing death.

  *   *   *

In our personal lives, as individuals, it is easy to say we're glad we can help and at the same time resent having to help. This may result in an attitude which hurts both the helped and the helper. Then we feel guilty. Musing about such a state of affairs, I forgot to put my bath towel where I could reach it easily. The wages of sin.

◁ June 18, 1992 ▷

Peeling an orange that had a thicker-than-usual rind caused me to recall a news item of the World War II era. I may still have the clipping somewhere, but some of my papers are in the attic and I have so many clippings not in the attic that it would take a long time to find the item. I hope my recollection is fairly accurate. I consider the incident, as I recall it, a little bit amusing, somewhat ironic and at the same time sad and regrettable.

This is what I remember: In the early days of atomic experimentation a shipload of pigs was taken to an area where atomic explosions were occurring. The pigs were fed oranges–lots of them–to see whether consumption of oranges might in some manner provide protection against radiation or fallout. The conclusion reached was that the oranges were helpful. However, since the pigs had eaten the whole oranges, peeling and all, no one knew which part of the oranges served the purpose. I think this could provide the basis of a sermon, or a political speech.

I recall being quite shocked in that same time period on learning that children in a European country were so hungry that they ate half-rotten oranges salvaged from discarded produce piles. I asked one of my journalism students to write an editorial about the tragic state of affairs. The editorial asking our East Bank High School students to refrain from wasting food appeared in a March, 1946 issue of *The Pioneer Chatterer*. I had no idea that in the future we would see rampant malnutrition and starvation on our television sets.

*   *   *

Occasionally I complain or moan about the fact that we can't seem to get around to building a "needed" addition to our house. However, I feel ashamed when I think of hundreds of people living in tents or huddled on hillsides or sleeping in the streets.

How would my perspective and the perspective of members of my family be altered if the only thing we could see as we look from the windows of our home would be the solid walls of another building almost touching ours? I wonder.

A long time ago I wrote a short piece saying that we could be thankful for even a tiny ray of sunlight that might reach us when circumstances are dire. This was broadcast as part of a devotional program. I find it easier to try to encourage others when I have a feeling of "sitting on the top of the world." It is more difficult to be hopeful when solutions are hard to find as they seem to be everywhere in the world today. There's a lot of work to be done.

❈ June 25, 1992 ❈

A *Time* magazine article about the weather mentions the fact that in 1928 storms in Nebraska produced hailstones the size of grapefruit. I was old enough in 1928 to know something of news events, but I don't recall grapefruit-size hailstones. Maybe our West Virginia newspapers didn't report that fact.

However, about that time I was concerned with adjusting to our family's move from one coal community to another. I had left behind a school where we had a special music teacher and a sandbox in the classroom where we were to build an Indian village. In my "new" school, in a community only a few miles away, but under the management of a different coal company, two grades of students were taught in one room, two students shared each desk and a bucket of water provided drinks. There was also an outdoor toilet. When the whole school played "Handy Over" at recess I was terrified, afraid that I might be the one to get hit by the ball.

I survived and in the sixth grade wrote fiction for the first time. My story was titled, "The Cake of Soap That Wanted To Grow Smaller."
*   *   *
Unwelcome Discovery: The kindest, wisest, most patient man may, in a moment of tension, revert to uttering an expression of blatant male chauvinism. Makes me wonder about the nature of things.
*   *   *
I haven't heard that anyone has reached a final, definite, scientifically–arrived–at conclusion concerning man's influence on the weather. I wonder about the possibility of reaching such a conclusion concerning weather changes.

Quite a few years ago men were creating additional snowfall in the western United States with the aim of providing more moisture where they thought it was needed.

This man-induced snowfall was produced in an area where avalanches had been occurring, but that didn't seem to be of great concern to the planners since they were chiefly interested in providing more moisture. (I suppose there may have been women scientists working on the project, but I don't know that there were.)

It does seem possible that our interference may at times cause unwelcome changes in nature. These thoughts about snow making occurred to me today, June 16, after I received a 1,406-page fall and winter catalog.

*   *   *

In an essay about women in politics Barbara Ehrenreich mentions the hope that no elected woman will feel obligated to prove her "manhood" by calling out the troops. I have noticed that sometimes women are quite warlike, but Ehrenreich's essay in *Time* merely offers hope, not a certainty.

❧ July 2, 1992 ☙

A teacher friend speaks of the frustration that occurs when students skip two of three classes, come late and leave early. This, I suppose, is the "new age" freedom. It's true that in some instances one might learn more studying "on his own" or researching, but if self-help education is what the students want they should enroll in special programs based on self-paced study. I am speaking of college level education, of course. Students below college level often cannot avoid missing school, a fact that is sad, but true.

It is very discouraging to a teacher to make a point which is a summation of what he has emphasized in previous sessions, when a look at the class tells him that some of the students were not present in those previous sessions and therefore probably don't know what he and other students who have attended regularly are talking about.

I am glad that my teacher acquaintance has some students whose attitude and accomplishments are rewarding. This perhaps will help prevent "the halls of learning" from suffering the loss of a gifted instructor.

When I returned to teaching after the absence of several years, I found it rather shocking to learn that students were quite surprised when asked to hand in work that they had been told to do outside of class. I was also shocked by the lack of 100% attendance in college classes. Is it, perhaps, time to consider reinstating a rule that was in effect when I was in college, enforced at my school and perhaps at other colleges? One could cut a class without expecting the heavens to fall, but there was definitely a limit to the number of times a student could cut classes with impunity. Perhaps the number of cuts allowed was based on the hours of credit for a particular class. I don't recall, but I do know that if you cut class more than the "allowed" number of times you could expect a failing grade or expulsion from that class.

    *   *   *

The professor in one of my classes–economics, I believe–was of the opinion that everything occurs in cycles. He mentioned seven-year cycles. I haven't tried to determine whether others agree with him. I've found economics too difficult a subject to intrigue me, and I did attend classes faithfully when I was in school. However, I have observed that pendulums swing–from one extreme to another, it seems.

When I was young we were seldom given a chance to think creatively or independently. (My sixth grade soap story was an exception.) We were not encouraged to question or argue. We memorized. I welcomed the trend toward allowing students or one's children to question and argue. I have recently decided that the pendulum has swung far enough. Sometimes I would almost welcome the return to "Children should be seen and not heard." Almost. I do long for moderation.

❧ July 9, 1992 ❧

Unable to sleep, I picked up a book published in 1923 and was surprised to find in the first fifty pages many quotations from speeches and writings of men who were speaking out vehemently against the slaughter and horrors of war. Apparently they didn't speak vehemently enough. The book is a copy of Elbert Hubbard's scrap book and, according to information written in the book, I purchased it in 1939. What surprised me was finding such a large number of men, not women, speaking of the folly and destruction of war.

I found protests against war made by Oscar Wilde, Victor Hugo, Louis Pasteur, Carlyle, Richard Le Gallienne, Leo Tolstoy, Charles Sumner, Joseph Dana Miller, William Ellery Channing and Benjamin Franklin. A powerful description of a soldier's thoughts as he sits in church is attributed to Wilhelm Lamszus. His words were not listed in the index under the subject *War*, perhaps because he closed his remarks by speaking of leaving the church and saying that he is not a coward. I found especially interesting Louis Pasteur's description of war as a force which "will sacrifice hundreds of thousands of lives to the ambition of a single individual."

*   *   *

During a college commencement service in 1939, I noticed that the girl walking beside me was crying. When I asked what was making her cry she told me that she had noticed that only her father was in the audience; her mother hadn't been able to come. The graduating student had been told beforehand that her parents might not have money enough for both of them to attend the ceremony, chiefly because they might not be able to buy presentable clothes for both. Depression years had caused hardships for a large family living on a small West Virginia farm. Yet, the girl was receiving a degree and, no doubt, some of her brothers and sisters would follow her in the pursuit of knowledge.

Before that graduation day I had observed a student in the dormitory bathroom scrubbing her shoes–not special tennis shoes, not Adidas or jogging shoes, but plain old brown leather oxfords which would probably be stiff and uncomfortable when they dried. Yet, the girl said she must scrub them because she had no other shoes and she couldn't stand the odor caused by constant wear. She wasn't happy about the situation, but she was in college, studying, regardless of means at her disposal.

I am inclined to think depression years made us try harder to pursue worthy goals, but I hesitate to say that hard times are beneficial. No one I knew died of starvation. If anyone near me ate from garbage cans I didn't know about it, and certainly in those days I saw no one sleeping on the streets in Huntington. But, they may have been; college students staying in dormitories weren't often on the streets at nights. Times have, indeed, changed.

Eighty issues of a daily newspaper appear in less than a fourth of one year. Eighty issues of *Hillbilly* appear in approximately a year and a half. Each reach thousands of readers and have existed for many years. The appearance of 80 issues of a monthly magazine that includes only essays, poetry and fiction seems less impressive but worth mentioning.

Hill and Valley magazine subsisted on donations and subscriptions only, but survived from October, 1977 to June, 1985. It could be called a desk-top publication since one person edited, put together and mailed it. I have spent hours this week sorting camera-ready copy prepared for the magazine. I have saved some pages, but discarded the majority, reluctantly. Since none of my own writing is in the book titled *Best of Hill and Valley, Editor's Choice*, I am saving some of the magazine's editorial pages for a scrapbook. These pages were a catch-all for announcements, corrections, and sometimes for the editor's pronouncements. Two I found today concerned something I had read.

I quoted, on the editorial page, a character from Edna Ferber's *Ice Palace* who said that it is childish to create more and more deadly weapons "to prevent and forestall" war. After reading *The Parsifal Mosaic* I mentioned an individual's helplessness as "events affecting nations are brought about by secret maneuvers, plots and counterplots." Then I wrote "But words do not die . . . and hope remains while wisdom is yet a possibility." (*Hillbilly* Editor Jim Comstock said it better in a 1974 publication: " . . . Truth thrives upon opposition . . . .")

As I type this after returning home from an evening drive over dangerously curving hillside streets, after approaching our home through dozens of cars, bravely and skillfully driven, I felt I should confess that I have no right to make pronouncements. I haven't driven a car for years and when I did I was not skillful. Perhaps I am completely outdated, but I persist.

While sorting pages of copy I have found some interesting facts. *Hill and Valley* had a small circulation, but copies went to many places: north to Canada; south to Texas; west to Nebraska, Oklahoma, California and Washington; east to several Atlantic coast states and farther still to one or more European countries. Libraries subscribed. Writers published in this 8 1/2" x 7" magazine included professors, public school teachers, housewives, ministers, steel workers, miners and clerks. Some saw their writing in print for the first time; others had been published elsewhere, but submitted some of their best work to *Hill and Valley*. Cost for the first year, $1,148.47; receipts that year, $1,208.18. Contributions of artists' work and the skill of copiers provided a presentable product. Eighty issues were welcomed by many. I enjoyed the work involved. I would encourage anyone who is twenty or thirty years younger than I to undertake publishing such a journal. It's needed. There are too few places where regional writers can see their fiction, poetry and nonfiction published.

❧ July 23, 1992 ☙

A reader wrote a letter to the editor of a daily newspaper criticizing a columnist for using the word *I* so many times. It's rather difficult to avoid using a personal pronoun when writing a personal opinion column.

*   *   *

The daughter who reads my scribblings faithfully when she receives copies pleased me when she made a special trip to a library to search for and find a copy of Sandburg's *Remembrance Rock* after I mentioned in a column that I'd like to find a copy. It's a weighty book. Carl Sandburg wrote very short poems, but he covered many pages when he turned to prose.

*   *   *

The trend toward exposing heroes' feet of clay is something to consider carefully. Do people in government try to preserve the favorable images of leaders who hold important roles and are influential in swaying public opinion? If so, do they sometimes get over-protective and jeopardize or sacrifice other people who, in their opinion, have less influence? *National Geographic's* recent article about General Douglas MacArthur is thought-provoking.

*   *   *

Although injuries and widespread looting occurred during a thirty-three hour blackout in New York City in July, 1977, only five homicides were reported during that period which included two nights. Usually, officials said, nine or ten homicides occur on one hot summer night. (That was in 1977.)

According to the Associated Press report, a policeman remarked that the looting may have saved lives. Another policeman said "It's hard to kill anyone when you got your hands filled with groceries." And doesn't that seem like food for thought?

*   *   *

After reading only 43 pages of *Remembrance Rock*, I've found two statements that impress me. They seem worth considering further. A character thinks that there is "no sorrow time does not touch and change and weave into something else." On another page four stumbling blocks to truth are listed. The list is attributed to Roger Bacon, who lived in the 13th century. The fourth hindrance is said to be "concealment of ignorance by ostentation of seeming wisdom."

*   *   *

This is my forty-sixth column of scribbling for this paper. Perhaps the time approaches when I should "cease and desist." *Remembrance Rock* was published by Harcourt Brace and Company, Inc. in 1948.

❡ July 30, 1992 ❢

For this week's scribbling, excerpts from one of a collection of essays. (This one, titled "A Momentary Perception," is about sunshine but not about the greenhouse effect.)

The woman stands on a rise at the edge of a sloping field. She has followed a path and pauses for a moment on her way. The day is sunny—bright and clean—and something about the atmosphere causes her to stand still, to gaze. For a moment she sees not only the view, but the future and the past, not intensely, only fleetingly. She sees the sunshine, the brightness symbolizing hope.

I don't know who she is. I know she wears a long skirt, caught by the breeze, and I think she must have a touch of white about her dress—snowy white, sun-bleached and dried. She isn't my mother, perhaps not my grandmother, possibly a great-great-grandmother I never knew. Her face glows serenely with an expression quite unlike those in stern-faced portraits . . . She gazes wide-eyed, but her face is relaxed, free of tension. Something about the view, the sunshine, the fleeting half-formed thoughts of the future gives her a boost, causing her to

85

proceed cheerfully along the path, continuing her tasks, performing work that, without a doubt, is hard, but satisfactory.

On such a sunny day in June she enters my mind. Fleetingly, I, too, glimpse sunshine existing in the future, cheering, nurturing . . . Momentarily, I have more strength. Momentarily I grasp hope, a feat not always easy, even for the staunchest idealist . . . Daily we see cruelty, hatred, war, indifference, and to each generation it may seem that it is more difficult than ever before to cling to ideals. Yet, hope persists.

. . . It's been said, "It's still a beautiful world." The imaginary person who occupies my mind during this bright sunshiny month glimpsed that beauty, continuing through the ages. At times I see it, too, with trust, hoping the sunshine will last, helping more than it harms, enabling us to see beauty existing around us, both outside and inside our houses, places of work, worship, and centers of learning . .

. . . And [we can] follow our ideals, even as we continue our daily humdrum or arduous work, hold tight to hope, keep striving. The brightness of a balmy summer day, or the welcome warmth of the sun on a winter day can be regarded as symbols of hope for mankind, or womankind, and keep us plodding along, stopping only occasionally for a look toward a brighter future. And sometimes, even if only momentarily, we feel a link, a bond, a continuity–a link with the past and the future that serves to give us a sense of the importance of our roles as individuals. My imaginary ancestress glimpsed this clearly as she stood at the edge of the field in the sunshine, and she smiled and continued on her way, knowing that her work was important.

*   *   *

And so endeth the essay. The original version appeared in Vol. IV of *Ansted Writers*, c. 1988.

In the next-to-the-last speech in Lillian Hellman's play, *Watch on the Rhine*, a character mentions flour paste, saying "I'm not put together with flour paste." I don't know that I've ever seen "flour paste" in print anywhere else. I was taught to make paste of flour and water when I was a child, and, although it didn't work perfectly, it would do in a pinch when no library paste was at hand. I suppose the character in the play is saying that she is stronger than she would be if she had been put together with flour paste rather than a better product.

In the last act of the play, Kurt Muller says " . . . The world is out of shape . . . when there are hungry men." He continues trying to explain the situation to his children, and he tells them they will live to see the day when the world is not out of shape. The play was published in 1941. The setting is 1940. I find it easier to understand now than at the time it was published, but I don't know that understanding the play contributes a great deal to alleviating hunger or preventing war. Kurt Muller's prediction has not come true–not yet. Is it worthwhile to mention that in some places today people would gladly eat flour paste?

For some unfathomable reason, thinking of the terms *flour paste* and *library paste* and *mucilage*, seldom heard today, causes me to recall the gold butterflies embroidered on my mother's chiffon camisole, and, strangely, the can of lemon drops obtained with a Larkin order. Long after the camisole was discarded, and when we were no longer taking Larkin orders, I still used flour paste occasionally. I recall making a "book" by pasting my Sunday School papers together, and my regret when I discovered that mice had eaten the pasted parts of the pages.

*   *   *

An attractive note card sent by a writer acquaintance featured a sketch of an abandoned gasoline filling station, surrounded by weeds. A sign on the building advertising Nehi gives us a clue to the age of the building. Seeing abandoned, small-business roadside enterprises always saddens me. Someone has hoped, planned, worked and then failed, often due to changing circumstances rather than because of poor effort. However, people who bravely opened the small restaurants or stores or filling stations didn't simply sit and daydream; they did something about their hopes and dreams. We can give them credit for trying.

In my answer to the person who sent the note, I mentioned that a friend and I, when we were about 13 years old, talked about a daydream of ours. Roadside tearooms had become a fad in small communities. The time was not favorable, but some of the small lunchrooms flourished bravely for a while. My friend and I talked of opening one someday, using furniture painted lavender and white. We had only a dim conception of the work that would be required, but that dream was short-lived and soon replaced by other plans. Wallace Stegner says we need dreams to "salve the wounds of living."

❧ September 24, 1992 ☙

In Sandburg's *Remembrance Rock*, page 468, I find the expression, "a smile meaningless as a thumbprint on a piecrust." I have 599 pages yet to read and the book is overdue. I want to finish the weighty novel. I'm intrigued and impressed by the amount of knowledge about our historic ancestors that I'm finding. I'm also surprised by some of the things I'm learning, but I think that author Carl Sandburg based his writing on research. I don't agree with his pie-crust evaluation, however. It is not meaningless to learn how to make a proper thumb printed pie-crust, one that looks the way you think it should look. I haven't completely mastered the art yet. My blackberry pies taste better than they look, sometimes.

*   *   *

A friend has asked me to mention in this column a booklet of poems written by a mutual friend. I considered doing so, but after thinking of the many people I know who have collections they would like to see distributed, I decided not to mention anyone by name. Instead, I suggest to readers that if you are so inclined it can be worthwhile to look at "thin volumes," sometimes self-published, that you may find in book stores such as Trans-Allegheny, or perhaps in the Hillbilly Book Shop. You may be surprised and delighted by some of your discoveries.

I was amazed to find an array of what seemed to be countless copies of such publications in Gotham Book Store in New York City several years ago. Stacks of thin paperback publications covered tables throughout the store, many of them showing evidence of having been there for quite some time. The manager accepted a few copies of the magazine I was publishing then, but if anyone ever purchased a copy of *Hill and Valley* there, I didn't learn about it. However, two writers from that area, one from upper New York State, submitted manuscripts and they may have seen the magazine on a dusty shelf at Gotham's.

Speaking of books, and of being surprised and delighted, I was surprised and delighted and well-fed, when treated by my thoughtful daughter-in-law to lunch at a book store in the Columbus area. Luncheon partakers are allowed to browse through the book store even while finishing their after-luncheon coffee, as I recall. (Perhaps that policy has been altered since I was entertained there.) I think the store is called Nickelby's, a prestigious name for a book store. Their black bean soup, a specialty, was delicious. Of course, I bought some books there, choosing from their used-book section. I merely wished for some of the new books, such as Rosamunde Pilcher's newest novel, but I managed to buy that one after I returned home.

Again speaking of books, I am always curious about books used as part of the decor in restaurants. They usually seem to be tantalizingly out of reach, on shelves so high that I can't read the titles.

P.S. Since I wrote this column, I finished *Remembrance Rock*, and gladly paid the overdue fine.

◁ October 1, 1992 ▷

A mother-daughter relationship is, sometimes, maybe often, a fragile thing. It's possible that when two in this category are both adults, working at housekeeping under the same roof, they get to know each other too well. Just a hastily formulated thought, for whatever it's worth, which may not be very much.

*　　　　　*　　　　　*

I have finally finished reading (on August 20) *Remembrance Rock*, Carl Sandburg's novel that acquaints us with people of the *Mayflower* era; people who lived through the American Revolution and those who didn't; people in America during the Civil War period; and people of the present generation. The story concludes with a section concerned with reaction in America to the dropping of atomic bombs. Being introduced to people from such a wide time span certainly involves a lot of getting-to-know-you. Nevertheless, I have been impressed again with the facts that our country is very young, and that those of us living in the United States today are much more fortunate than we can easily realize.

I think it's possible that our youngest grandson may have very close ties to the earliest European colonists who settled here. One of the two vegetables that he eats willingly is corn. However, I don't think he would respond happily to a diet of corn meal mush such as that which kept many colonists alive during the harsh winters they endured.

From *Remembrance Rock:*

Page 602: "Love of country is a holiness that comes and goes . . . those too sure of it better beware."

*   *   *

Lloyd C. Douglas' green-light theory, which I first learned about many years ago, helped sustain my hope for mankind (and womankind) for a while, whenever I had time to think about it. (Caring for five children can be time-consuming.) I had read Douglas' books in the 1930's and was cheered by the idea he expressed about the progress of civilization. Sometimes we are halted on a plateau, he said, and have to wait a while, but eventually we get the green light and can go upward.

These days I am not quite so idealistic as in the past. We seem to be besieged by forces that halt any progress toward the goal of improving civilization. Injustice, failure, frustration and confusion surround us. Yet, when we think of the past (longer ago than when I was young), even going only as far back as the Middle Ages, when people might be tested by being forced to thrust their hands into a pot of boiling water to determine whether they were guilty or innocent, then it does seem that slowly and surely we have made some progress in a climb upward. We can hope for more frequent green light signals.

*   *   *

I hope no one thinks I intended to write *steel miners* in a July column rather than *steel workers* and *coal miners*. I'm mentioning it, just in case.

❧ October 8, 1992 ☙

I am not sure why going to a reunion of high school graduates whom I taught when I was young has been so much more enjoyable than attending my fiftieth year college reunion. The 1942 graduates of East Bank High School invited teachers to their fiftieth reunion, and my husband and I enjoyed a pleasant evening spent with them. People attending knew me when I was important to them because I was a teacher. People attending my college graduation class reunion had forgotten all about how important I was when I was in college, if they ever knew! It was difficult for them to recall that I was in college when they were! Perhaps that explains the different levels of enjoyment.

One person at the college reunion kept repeating my name, trying to remember that I had existed. I remember her. She was fortunate in that her table-waiting job in our college dormitory paid more than other work available. I remember how she looked in her white uniform. Waiting tables was strenuous. I'm sure she had little energy left for dabbling in activities I made time for, such as college politics.

The part-time work I did during my last two years in college paid thirty cents an hour. I was lucky to get it. During my junior year I was paid by the National Youth

92

Administration to work in the dean's office, but the national organization could not pay me during my senior year because my father, paralyzed by a stroke, was still being paid a small monthly sum by the coal company he had worked for. Miss Lucy Prichard, Latin professor, came to the rescue as she so often did, and paid me to tutor some of her students.

*   *   *

Some books are worth rereading and sometimes seem more meaningful after a lapse of several years. Seeing the movie *Mutiny on the Bounty* made me want to read the book. I have a battered paperback copy, but don't know whether or not I've read it. Can't get to it just now; I'm reading two other books. One is Denise Giardina's *Storming Heaven* which I'm rereading to prepare for a discussion in November. My first reading was probably too biased, too defensive. I have a new Rosamunde Pilcher book which my daughter bought, but I'm saving it for a very special time. And, speaking of books and movies, I can't recall whether I once read *The Last of the Mohicans*, but I think I'd like to see the new movie version.

I probably won't read much of anything today. Bowls of tomatoes and the last of the garden peppers are sitting in our kitchen, and I've opened a cookbook to two recipes for chow-chow. When my husband brought the tomatoes and peppers in, he asked if I think we could make some chow-chow. Perhaps we might; perhaps if he's not too busy scraping and repainting gutters and eaves, he may help with chopping ingredients or take time to go buy more vinegar. One recipe calls for 2 cups of vinegar and another calls for 2 quarts, each with the same amount of tomatoes, and I've never made chow-chow before! Perhaps I should just read a book.

Occasionally I reach a point where I have nothing to say. The small amount of fall housecleaning I've finished this week has not inspired any great and lofty thoughts, but has given me a small measure of satisfaction. Who said, "It's better to light a candle than to curse the darkness?" Confucius or Lin Yutang? I'm inclined to agree with that statement. Even the shabbiest furniture looks better when clean, and cleaning half a room is better than not cleaning any. Right?

Having thought of Lin Yutang, I decided to look at the two of his books which I have, purchased many years ago, probably in the 1940's, according to the reprint dates. The titles are intriguing: *Between Tears and Laughter* and *With Love and Irony*. Pearl Buck wrote the introduction for one, explaining that Lin Yutang was at that time an essayist who had written bravely, with wit, for a Chinese periodical. His essays also appeared in such American publications as *Cosmopolitan* and *New York Times*. Ms. Buck said that Lin Yutang is [was] a genius.

Considering the fact that I was very busy in the 1940's I doubt that I read all the essays in the two books, but I find that I have underlined certain statements. Turning the pages I find many that set me thinking, sometimes with amusement, when the author mentions human foibles; sometimes sadly, when he speaks of war. Examples:
"If Confucius and Dr. Johnson [Samuel] had met, they would have smiled and understood each other perfectly."
"The balance of power theory has kept Europe in periodic bloodshed . . . for the last few centuries."
"Soap has become democratic."

"The Chinese believe that . . . when there are too many soldiers there can be no peace."

" . . . the greatest force produces the greatest hatred."

" . . . I felt very happy in spite of myself."

*   *   *

I am looking forward with pleasure to two activities planned for this week. One, attending a dinner arranged by the West Virginia Humanities Council honoring Editor Jim Comstock who will receive the 1992 Humanities Award. The second occasion, being entertained by my former college roommate in a town only a few minutes' drive away. Regardless of the short distance, we see each other seldom. I wonder why our present-day lifestyles leave so little time for visiting, and why it is that I don't know people who live less than a block away from our home. Lin Yutang could write an essay based on the question.

*   *   *

The back-page essay in the October 12 issue of *Time* speaks of a costly addiction and uses the phrase "toxic dependency on militarism." The writer says "Weapons firms are notoriously loath to beat their swords into plowshares . . . It's easier to mail out the pink slips."

❧ October 22, 1992 ❧

A 1988 headline caught my attention as I sorted papers: SUSPECTED REBELS KILL 17 FOR VOTING. I won't name the country where the killing occurred. In the ensuing four years that country could have vanished, or the rebels may have become people in power and, by some odd quirk, voting may have become respectable in that location. So much turmoil and upheaval exist today in so many places that I don't feel the need to try to find out what has happened recently in that particular country.

I do, however, feel impelled to comment on the possibility of hope for the world, a hope which grows dim at times. Pollyanna and I can be glad that in the United States of America today we don't expect to hear that any of our countrymen lose their lives because they have voted. Granted, people seem to grow belligerent at times concerning a voter's choice of candidate, but people often argue over relatively unimportant issues. I certainly hope that no one in our country will be shot for voting–not this year. I hear that a very large voter turnout is expected.

*   *   *

My chow-chow, mentioned previously, made from a guessed-at-recipe, was pronounced edible, although I think it was closer to being piccalilli than chow-chow. The garden tomatoes are almost gone, so I won't have to worry about making chow-chow any more this year.

*   *   *

Speaking of disagreements, I wish someone would think of a way to prevent people on discussion panels from interrupting each other. It would be necessary to implement a system to limit each person's allotted time for speaking. It's really difficult to gain any information when three people are talking at the same time. I don't intend to ask children who have been told not to interrupt what they think of what they see if they happen to tune in any of the adult debates on television.

*   *   *

I was taught that newspaper headlines require capitalization, but I really hadn't noticed, until I looked carefully at the 1988 headline, that this rule is not always followed. How easily we adjust to change, sometimes! And sadly, how often we accept rule breaking and fail to question the reason for the act.

*   *   *

When I was young, one of my favorite quotations told me that a happy person carries his own weather with him. I liked this statement because to me it seems rather useless to complain about something we can't change. It's unpleasant if someone grumbles and complains if it rains on the day of the picnic, and it's better if we adjust and make a game of an indoor picnic. However, since scientists and others now tell us that what we do can affect the weather, we could, after the in-house picnic, write polite letters to our congressmen, complaining about the weather. They might do something as a result, and they probably would at least spend some time talking about such an important subject.

❧ October 29, 1992 ☙

"It takes a heap o' livin' in a house to make it home." These words by Edgar Guest have been in my mind this week and not easily dismissed. There may be a connection to memories of my mother's fall housecleaning which was thorough and effective. However, her home was never cluttered. It was not bare; there were books and magazines, but they didn't cover every available surface and they were not interspersed with countless objects–novelities, vases, boxes, sea shells, pine cones.

How do people manage to get rid of souvenirs, gifts, tokens that have been around for a while? I put some in drawers, sometimes; sometimes I take them out again. I really don't want to lose them. They represent people, ideas, experiences, and so they remain to be dealt with at cleaning time. I have made a little progress in the matter of ridding the house of papers. I have probably discarded enough paper to make a small bonfire, but I have more.

Looking for the "Heap o' Livin' " poem, I had no success for the first few minutes because I was sure that the words were written by James Whitcomb Riley. Luckily, I found a copy of Guest's Home poem in a scrapbook in a trunk. I found something else there which was rather disconcerting. An unidentified clipping, with content that made it sound as if it came from an education journal and was intended to give advice to teachers, included the sentence, "It is better to light a candle than to curse the darkness." Whoever composed that sentence is not identified in the list of six statements appearing under the title "In a Nutshell." Can any reader help me identify the candle quote? When I talked about it in a previous column, I mentioned Confucius as the possible source.

Our house would certainly qualify as a home under the "heap o' livin' " category. I've often said it should have movable walls so that adjustments could be quickly made to allot space when the number of people living in the house increases or decreases. Incidentally, we're finally getting another small room added, with two sons working to try to get a roof up before snow flies in our valley. And, I do realize that I should be ashamed of being reluctant to clean house and of voicing complaints about the size of the house, considering the tragic fact that thousands are homeless.

*   *   *

In her latest novel, *Murder at the Pentagon*, published by Random House, Margaret Truman speaks courageously of events of 1990-92, including Desert Storm. Pentagon problems, of a type that may surface in the future, are part of the interesting story.

Note: While writing a previous column my fingers may have typed letters without specific instructions from my mind. That can happen. Or, kind and skillful copy editors may have access to word lists I haven't seen. Three dictionaries in our house list seldom as an adverb without the additional *ly*.

⚜ November 5, 1992 ⚜

According to fiction I've read, some of the people of China living in the Middle Ages thought the Europeans whom they chanced to meet needed to bathe more often. I think it may be a historical fact that one of England's queens had only two baths in her life. I recall seeing a picture of that queen wearing a voluminous white bejeweled dress. I don't know whether the picture was supposed to show her as she appeared before or after her second bath.

It surely must have been very cold in castles, and outdoor bathing in a stream would have been even more uncomfortable. However, a source I consulted mentioned that during the sixteenth century in some places people avoided bathing because of religious beliefs. I also learned, while looking for information on bathing, that Louis XIV of France took a bath once a year and that some great ladies usually washed their hands and faces once or twice a week.

It seems that some Christians considered the Roman system of bathing immoral. It was not until 1755 that baths built by Romans in England during the first century were excavated. Although they had been developed with efficient heating and cooling systems, they had been buried for centuries. It is difficult to persuade someone to take a bath who doesn't want to bathe. (Ask any mother.)

New England temperatures endured by early colonists in this country and primitive accommodations would not always foster an eagerness for frequent use of water, but somewhere along the way the saying that cleanliness is next to godliness became generally popular. Surely more shampoo is purchased in America today than ever before in the history of our country and shampoo is used lavishly where people are fortunate enough to have water and money. I think often of the dust, discomfort and inconvenience endured by people traveling by stage coach or covered wagon and admire their tenacity.

*   *   *

This week's news tells us that in England coal miners are alarmed about the closing of mines and in America a 1931 musical about politics is revived and being well received. This encourages me to think that my play with music, about coal mining people in the 1950's, may still have a chance. Luckily, the play is not dead. An adaptation was performed in May and actor David Selby has agreed to listen to a tape of the music.

*   *   *

Food for thought? People of each country or race are inclined to think themselves and their accomplishments superior, forgetting that people in other countries have made worthy accomplishments. New inventions, new processes are accepted and used and credit is not always given to the primary source. The magnetic compass, for example, was probably first used in China long before western people knew of its existence. Sometimes methods that seem new to us have forerunners in other countries and earlier times. Ancient Romans "conditioned" their homes by circulating heated air between double walls.

❁ November 12, 1992 🕬

I have remembered clearly that in 1935 my letter to *Ladies' Home Journal* magazine asking advice about clothes for college was answered in detail, with replies made to questions I had asked about the few clothes I had available and how I could supplement them. The staff person who wrote the letter even enclosed a clipping from a newspaper ad suggesting what type of hat I might find suitable. I have remembered this clearly because I have included the reply and illustration in a scrapbook. The friendly comments in the letter gave me courage and I weathered my first year in college very well. I was never ashamed of the cloth overshoes I bought for 75¢ even though they did look rather awkward–rather, they made my feet look awkward, and I was pleased that my aunt made a coat for me from an old coat of my mother's. How lucky I was!

I had completely forgotten another instance of receiving help from a nationally circulated magazine, but a box of souvenirs brought down from the attic yesterday informed me. During World War II, preparing for a trip to New York, I wrote to *Esquire* magazine to ask about hotels. That letter, too, was answered in detail, listing prices, locations and advice. Are there nationally circulated magazines today whose staff members would give such personalized advice? Perhaps. I have received a few personal letters about manuscripts I've submitted.

This reminds me that I once thought my life would be perfect if I could have an opportunity to work for *Ladies' Home Journal*. Now I know that I might have starved in New York. Also, I know that life provides compensations. More than fifty years after I aspired to become a famous writer living in New York, I am privileged to write for *The West Virginia Hillbilly*, a respected, widely circulated newspaper. For this I am truly grateful.

The letter I received from Lawton Mackall, columnist for *Esquire*, is dated July 26, 1943. Mr. Mackall told me which of the hotels I had asked about provided dance music and he quoted the discount available for service men. At the Roosevelt a room with double bed and private bath would cost $6.50, less a 25% discount. At the Bristol Hotel luncheon was from 70¢ up and dinner from $1.40.

Included in my box of souvenirs were four pages of a December, 1940 comic strip featuring "Terry and the Pirates." I'm not sure why these were saved. I think that later, when my brother was overseas, he said that he and other naval pilots enjoyed that particular series.

    *   *   *

November 4, 1992. Was it Abraham Lincoln who said, "You can't fool all of the people all the time"?

    *   *   *

While I was still in college I had an opportunity to write a column for *The Cabin Creek Courier*, which existed briefly. I titled the column "Scribblings of a Cabin Creeker." A college professor who read samples of the column said it was too didactic. If we don't have thoughts we want to express, why write?

৯ November 26, 1992 ৶

I think I may be guilty. I have written something that is not true–at least, not completely true. I did it innocently. Apparently my memory betrayed me. In the Scribbling column appearing in the March 5 issue, I said that I had never seen French-fried sweet potatoes on a menu anywhere and that I would like to know how they are prepared. I had learned about such a dish while reading a very old letter.

Recently, I spent a good deal of time sorting recipes, I was looking for and I found a special recipe for a Christmas roast which includes a sauce flavored with apricots and prunes. We had thought that recipe was lost. (It's a favorite of at least one member of the family!)

During the search I unfolded a newspaper clipping dated November 25, 1981, which had probably been saved for the pumpkin pie recipe included in an article by *The Charleston Gazette's* Delmer Robinson. The other recipe in the article was for fried sweet potatoes! These were not French-fried, however. Perhaps that fact exonerates me. Then, too, perhaps my eyes skipped over the potatoes and concentrated on the pumpkin pie.

Trivial? Yes, but I am thinking of the fact that at times we look at something without really seeing it. Perhaps this provides safety for our minds which are bombarded with so many sights, sounds and printed words. Enough said on this subject!

*   *   *

Marco Polo has told us of people living long ago in the Far East who cooled their houses with ventilators and knew how to make powdered milk to carry on journeys. He also tells of certain other practices of these ancient people which we consider barbaric and deplorable today. Will a time come when our good accomplishments are noted and then compared regretfully with some of our habits (such as fighting wars) which will seem barbaric to people in a future age?

The powdered milk processed by people living approximately seven hundred years ago, according to my copy of *Travels of Marco Polo*, could be mixed with water by a traveler to sustain him on his way. M. P. also tells us how they made the powder, but I decided against repeating his explanation here. Do you recall that in this modern age we've had a problem with powdered milk not correctly used by consumers, resulting in the illness of children?

* * *

Lecomte duNouy has said that the true symbol of civilization is the development of human dignity. He reminded us in his book, *Human Destiny**, that a moral code consisting of a few basic rules appeared "as if by miracle" in the four corners of the world. These rules, in his opinion, must accompany any mechanical transformations if we are to become truly civilized. Inventions have become the false symbols of civilization, according to duNouy.

*Published by Longmans, Green and Co., 1947.

⍒ December 3, 1992 ✎

I have read that Jenny Lind, the Swedish soprano, toured the United States during 1850 to 1852, under the management of P. T. Barnum. I have also read, somewhere, in a source I can't find, that while on tour she insisted that she have her own private accommodations at each location. As a result, according to whatever it was I read and can't find, hastily constructed buildings were made for her, of a type that came to be called Jenny Lind buildings.

* * *

Before my book about coal mining and coal miners was published in 1981, I clipped and saved every mention I found of anything related to coal mining. I have also clipped and saved many such references since 1981. Result: Boxes and boxes and stacks and envelopes filled with such clippings. *Coal and People* is now out of print and I am attempting to sort and discard many of these collected materials. Today as I worked at this task I noticed that I have many news items concerning "proposed" laws, reforms, controls, safety measures and reclamation provisions, but I seldom found, in this particular box, notices that laws have been enacted, reforms have been made or compromise reached. I found few follow-up stories. It's possible that results may be in the special collection of notes used in writing the book, or it's possible that when proposals are defeated, headlines are not very large and I have overlooked such news. However, I have found in these surplus materials reports of failure to abide by regulations and instances of reduction of penalties. It seems that similar problems resurface year after year.

*   *   *

A reader of this column, Ted Kyle, recommends Arthur Gordon's book, *A Touch of Wonder.* In the epilogue of his book Mr. Gordon describes the light of small candles which cannot be conquered by the darkness in the world. Also, Bill Smith of Williamstown, who says he likes all of *Hillbilly's* columns, has written concerning the candle-lighting quotation mentioned in a previous column. (You may have read Mr. Smith's letter in the November 12th issue.) He enlisted the help of librarians and found that Adlai Stevenson spoke of Eleanor Roosevelt when he talked of lighting candles as an activity preferred to cursing the darkness.

*   *   *

Tis the season for the production of "Everyman," the very, very old morality play that tells us good deeds are important, something Scrooge is supposed to have learned about 300 years later. (The University of Charleston Theater presented "Everyman" this month, with five performances providing opportunity for varied audiences.) We present-day mortals may want to pause to consider, very seriously, the nature of our good deeds. It is regrettable that we concentrate on helping others chiefly in the holiday seasons rather than during the whole year, but–helping once is better than not helping at all. Right?

≈ December 10, 1992 ≈

I like hearing the distant sound of carpenter's hammers. The sound is pleasant to my ears and reminiscent of the past. It's especially pleasing to hear such a sound today, because this happens only when my house is free of noise, when there is no television blaring, no household appliances operating, no telephone ringing. Then I can hear the peaceful industrious sound coming from my neighbor's property. I'm not sure why I liked the sound in the past, but I remember writing a poem that mentioned the sound of building. Shortly after I thought about the pleasant sound of hammering, I saw people on television fleeing from oncoming fighters and I learned that the conquerors were burning homes as they advanced. Our complacent musings are easily pierced as television shows us what the real world is like for other people. My pleasure on a long-ago afternoon was not marred by thinking of disasters affecting people in other countries. Yet, as sensitive people we were often aware of tragedy, even though we had no television. I recall seeing my grandmother sadly, seriously shaking her head as she read of mishaps in the news. She didn't understand, she said, how people could be so cruel. Yet, she surely had been aware of tragedies in the lives of people she knew. I remember hearing her speak of two things that seemed most regrettable to her. She had heard people tell of soldiers or renegades traveling through the country during or after the Civil War who ripped open feather pillows and scattered the feathers. The second act she spoke of at length happened when she lived near a family whose conversations she could hear easily. The wife in the family was a late sleeper and on many mornings her husband could be heard begging her to get up and cook his breakfast. Such a state my grandmother couldn't understand. She also mentioned once, almost in a whisper, that she had heard that coffins were lined up in rows at a railroad station during a time of labor trouble.

*   *   *

Speaking of problems resurfacing, I was somewhat amused at seeing certain words recurring so often as I turned through a college text used by one of our sons a number of years ago. A *History of the Roman People* discusses problems of the Roman Empire from its beginning and throughout the years to the fifteenth century. Over and over the word *taxes* appears. Taxes were lowered, taxes were increased. Taxes were removed, people were exempt from taxes or new taxes were levied. The phrases are very familiar to us in the U. S. and our country is only a little more than 200 years old. As I scanned the book I looked for references to subjects most interesting to me, including construction projects. I noticed that libraries appeared in various parts of the world. People in all the continents are more closely related than we usually remember.

*   *   *

In the twentieth century Americans have been accused of seeming arrogant as they travel in other lands. At home we often notice "foreign" accents and noses of different shapes and forget that people "not like us" have rich cultural backgrounds. It seems we need "the long view" as we consider the development of the human race.

❧ December 17, 1992 ❧

Going to war for peace? I first heard such a paradoxical expression in the 1930's when I was told that World War I was the war fought to end all wars. I hoped that was true; I suppose I believed it was a fact, or that I could help make it come true. I made a very emotional high school assembly speech declaring that we would "war no more." I haven't felt embarrassed as I recall that speech, but I haven't made another one like it.

Boris Pasternak wrote in *Dr. Zhivago* " . . . what has for centuries raised men above the beast is not the cudgel but an inward music." Other words from Pasternak's novel that call for thinking: "All women are mothers of great men–it isn't their fault if life disappoints them later." I notice that he doesn't say "if their sons disappoint them." He says "if life disappoints them." It seems likely that in some cases both mothers and sons are disappointed. (By life?)

    *   *   *

It is heartening (heartwarming) to attend a Christmas dinner party arranged for employees and to see younger men, now working, take time to talk with retirees who helped train them or worked with them in years past. A spirit of camaraderie made enjoyable the APCO dinner my husband and I attended.

In our two-family household we take turns cooking. My husband is not regularly scheduled, but he likes to "chip in" sometimes, preparing something considered a specialty of his, such as baked stuffed fish or sweet and sour pork, or venison steak or zucchini casserole. (I haven't had much success recently with saying, "The kids think your spaghetti is better than mine." However, he likes to get up early on Sunday and prepare breakfast foods which are left on the stove to tempt or treat anyone who appears.) We have gotten in the habit of omitting a large family-sit-down noon or evening Sunday meal, usually subsisting on left-overs or individually prepared snacks. I like eating in restaurants, but I feel somewhat guilty in a restaurant on Sunday, thinking that the restaurant staff members need a day of rest. My grandmother always said that "any extra work" you do on Sunday, such as mending, will never turn out right, but I don't think she would ever let anyone go hungry on Sunday.

*   *   *

Today's inventions are mind-boggling, for me, at least. I still don't understand radio. I have a dim understanding of what makes planes fly, but I avoid thinking about space ships and guided missiles. Looking at a new book about the *Titanic*, with its photographs of the huge vessel, amazed me, as I considered the boldness of men who dared to put such a heavy entity on the sea, expecting it to float. Men have accomplished great feats. Nothing, however makes less the wonder and awe produced by considering the fact that every person's fingertips are different from every other person's, so that each of us can be identified and acknowledged as a separate special individual.

❁ December 24, 1992 ❂

I have mentioned previously in this column Jackson Stover, who taught, coached and directed recreation in West Virginia for many years. During the last years of his life he wrote stories based on what he saw and heard as he grew up on Coal River near Colcord. One of these stories was accepted for publication shortly before he died; this pleased him very much. Members of his family have talked of having the stories published, but somehow most of them have been lost. Just recently I found I have copies of two of his tales which he copied for me at his home in Fernandina Beach in 1965. (Incidentally, he was fond of *The West Virginia Hillbilly* and saved copies for me to bring back to

W.Va.) While Mr. Stover, my uncle, was a very young man he worked for a while at the Y.M.C.A. at Decota on Cabin Creek, possibly before he was graduated from Davis and Elkins College. One of the two stories I have includes these lines, probably based on facts concerning the Y.M.C.A. in the coalfields:

"He went down to the settlement at the forks of the river [creek?] to find work. He was lucky in finding a job the very first day, not in the mine. He was hired to help repair and paint the old Red Rabbit saloon building. You see, the company wanted to do something for the benefit of the young people, something to get them to like the place and to make for a better community spirit; and consequently, they hoped to attract family men to the jobs through the programs set up and operated for the people in that area. Thus was established the first industrial Y.M.C.A. in the bituminous coal fields in this country. Of course, the anthracite fields had several Y's in operation in Pennsylvania. This first Y in our area became the community center and through the activities it sponsored it touched the lives of nearly everyone in the settlement." So he wrote as an introduction to a story about a young man who played baseball. I can vouch for the importance of the Y.M.C.A at Decota because I enjoyed activities there as I grew up.

The second story is titled "Chestnut Hunting With Gramps," and part of it follows:

"Again all was silence except the rustling of the wind in the leaves around the campfire and Gramps seemed to be in a deep study for a while. Then at last he said, "I've been thinkin' some sorrowful thoughts about who would be takin' you boys into the hills, an' on trips such as this, or fox huntin' or rampin' or sengin', or who would larn ye about climbin' fools' hill, which is a part of every boy's growin' up . . . I want you sprouts to be the backbone of these hills . . . Now don't think I am talkin' about gettin rich–I'm talkin' about bein' MEN . . . Some [of the sprouts] in the quietness out here under the stars learned to live; some found a dream an' followed it to manhood an' success; some didn't.

" ' . . . Respect, that's what I want for you. I want people to respect an' honor ye cause ye will stand up an' prove your worth. Like these hills ye will be landmarks to make folks know that ye are constant an' endurin', that ye will be ready when wanted and able when needed.' "

$$*\qquad\qquad *\qquad\qquad *$$

Arthur Gordon, not Arthur Graham, wrote *A Touch of Wonder*. I am grateful to Mr. Theodore Kyle for helping me correct the error.

☙ December 31, 1992 ❧

Several years ago a one-word poem won a prize and national attention. The subject was light. I don't recall the title, but you can guess the identity of the one word, which I think may have been followed by exclamation marks. Undoubtedly, some people were indignant; some scoffed, but as I appreciate spots of sunlight on a winter day or admire leaf-patterned sunlight in another season I consider the one-word poem suitable. Light is beautiful; light is valuable; it is very welcome after a long, dark night. (Of course, I didn't write it! I should be so lucky!).

$$*\qquad\qquad *\qquad\qquad *$$

Reversal
(Written after salvaging a discarded notebook)
The paper lies blank, discarded, rescued from the trash.

Pages and pages now wait for me, and I wait–dejected,
disappointed, discarded. No, it isn't true.
Didactic, I survive and fill a space with words,
but I dare not count the empty pages.
Didactic, they challenge me.

    *   *   *

 If you burn a pan of potatoes, as I did last week, just
enough to cause you to lose only a little of the food, but
enough to require scraping scrubbing, rubbing and
polishing, the final result may be pleasing. Behold a pan
that looks like new–on the inside! A favorite story I used to
read to tenth grade English classes described the mother in
the story as being the sort of person whose kitchen pots and
pans were as clean on the outside as on the inside. I feel a
bit guilty when I think of the description.

Remnants

A bit of tinsel, a dry needle from the Christmas pine,
one delicate icicle–these persist throughout the year.
We clean the house, pay the carpet cleaners, move furniture.
But in March or maybe June, or later still,
A scrap of Christmas is found–under a cushion,
behind a bookcase, or in the middle of the floor,
surprisingly appearing there, these remnants of Christmas,
reminders of Yuletide peace, telling us something.

    *   *   *

Wishing, 1984

I want it to be Christmas again. I want the day to go more
slowly. I want to see all the faces, and then sit and watch
and listen.

I want it to be Christmas again. I promise that somehow I
will move slowly, speak softly, all day, and when someone
laughs I'll be able to hear.

When someone smiles I want to see; if a child is tired, perhaps hold that one on my knee.
I want it to be Christmas again.

Our house is quieter this year, someone said. I reminded him that everyone is older–eight years older than when I wrote "Wishing." I have been able to sit and watch and listen, thanks to the tremendous help of some family members who are eight years older. That's progress! "Remnants" and "Wishing" were previously published in *Still no Theme.*

        ❧ January 7, 1993 ☙

The first paragraph in the first of my "Scribblings and More," published in this paper August 22, 1991, was as follows: "Space in a newspaper is important. Being given an opportunity to have words you have written considered for publication is a privilege, and at the same time, humbling. Knowing your thoughts may be read by many knowledgeable adults produces shyness, at least for me. When I first wrote a column for a weekly newspaper, many years ago, I was so shy that I asked permission to simply call myself a scribbler, and my name was not published."

During the years since that early venture, a variety of my efforts has been published in a variety of publication. I've been paid for some of them, including a series of twelve excerpts from one of my books, published in a magazine with a circulation of 250,000. I understand very well, however, that not all writing is pleasing to all readers.

Dr. Robert Newman said in a back-cover comment for a book I edited that the magazine which I had edited and published "reflected the heights and depths of our human condition . . . gently nudging and prodding us . . ." I suppose that description might be applied to the columns I have written. I cling to the belief that as civilized people we have made progress through the ages and that with effort we can continue to do so. Although this belief is battered and wobbly at times, I still think that Pollyanna had the right idea.

In addition, I am, and always have been, eager to portray the positive aspects in the lives of coal mining people, and I have, in this column, from time to time, mentioned historical facts related to life in coal communities.

When I first asked Editor Jim Cornstock if I might submit sample columns to be considered as a regular feature, he said that I might, but he said he wasn't sure how long he would be editing the paper. I am most grateful for the opportunity I have had, and I am very appreciative, too, of the fact that some readers have let me know that they read the column.

I offer sincere good wishes to the new owner-editors, Russell and Carolee McCauley. This includes the wish that the paper will prosper under their direction and continue to be the kind of paper that the majority of the readers and subscribers want.

*   *   *

A quick look at the January 4th issue of *Newsweek* makes mentioning Pollyanna and hope for the world seem almost ridiculous. Beginning with the cover, which features war crimes in Bosnia, I found nothing to be glad about in 37 of the 55 pages. In a lighter vein, however, a small news item on page 8 tells of a hotel in Sweden built of ice and snow. For a fee of $51 dollars you may sleep on a bed of snow, covered with reindeer hides–before April, when the hotel will probably melt. Staying there might serve to make you forget for a while all the strife, suffering and discomfort elsewhere in the world.

❧ January 14, 1993 ❧

As Long as There Is Hunger–could this be a title for a book, an essay, a sermon? I think about the expression and find it evokes two possibilities. At first, we may complete the statement by saying, " . . .there will always be war, or hatred, or trouble." On the other hand, we may think, "As long as there is hunger for truth, for fairness, for mercy, for the good–as long as there is such hunger, we may be motivated to try to promote these values, rather than giving up and saying, "It's no use." (As Long as Hunger Exists is more concise, but I like the first wording better. That relates to a problem writers have–being overly fond of what they have said.)

*   *   *

A letter written to a daily paper expressed the opinion that it is useless and a waste of space to print quotations from other sources. The writer says he is looking for new thoughts. Yet, so much of what has been said in the past, even though wise and worthwhile, has been ignored. It seems we learn slowly. Often, what is hailed as being new was first said long ago. An "old thought" could affect a reader's mind in a new way.

*   *   *

Susan Faludi, author of *Backlash*, states in an article in *Newsweek* that she considers the expression "for women" more significant than the expression "year of the women," the latter seeming to imply either that 1992 may be the last chance for improving conditions or that enough has been accomplished.

*   *   *

The sun is shining; fishing tackle is being inspected and refurbished. Trout stocking time is here and soon there will be one less person in our house during part of the week. There is no need for me to say what I think of a sport that includes, some of the time, releasing and throwing back part of the catch. No one has convinced me that hooks don't hurt the fish, but I like and respect the fisherman who goes forth from our house. Since he is very patient concerning my scribbling I must be patient and try not to worry too much because the sun always seems to go down faster than he expected on fishing days. Besides, the contents of our freezer verify the fact that he brings home a substantial part of the catch. It will be nice, however, if our water heater is working again before the fishing season is over.

Postcript: On the day I wrote the first draft of the above the water heater was fixed by the "old fisherman" and one of our sons. I'm grateful, and I think again of the cap I bought as a gift. It says that people who go fishing are free, for a little while, because when fishing they have no worries, no clock, no work and no phone. Everyone needs to rest, sometimes.

January 21, 1993

I have just finished reading a book which I bought in 1942. There are several reasons why I might have failed to read any book in 1942. Fifty years ago I was 24 years old and very busy. *Bright to the Wanderer* is a novel and not at all hard to read. I enjoyed it, but a story about members of a family who left the United States in 1781 and their progress and struggles in Canada until 1840 wasn't

116

intriguing enough in 1942 to cause me to put aside other interests and keep reading.

Reading the book now has made me realize that I know very little about Canada. We have spent time in Canada and learned a little about the country and some of the people, but I didn't know enough about it before we went. I tried to find a place that had both a magnificent fishing spot and a place for the children to swim. My numerous long distance calls didn't achieve that goal. We spent most of the time in a cottage quite a distance from the shore of Lake Nipissing. Before we returned home I discovered a few things I hadn't expected: (1) Labels in a grocery store were written in French. (2) It was so cold at night that we nearly froze trying to play miniature golf. (3) Logs may be placed in a motel swimming pool to keep the pool from cracking. That's what we were told. At any rate, the logs prevented the children from swimming in the only pool we had access to on the way back to the states.

Bruce Lancaster, author of *Bright to the Wanderer,* published by Little, Brown and Co., incorporated historic facts and figures in his story. Intrigued, I checked the encyclopedia for information about William Lyon Mackenzie, who inspired some Canadians to rebel against British government as it was represented by a faction called "The Compact." I learned that a ship named *Caroline,* moored on the United States side of a river, and used by Canadians to further their rebellion, was, indeed, set on fire and sent over Niagara Falls by people opposing their action.

I did not realize, before reading this book, that very close ties existed between people of Canada and the people of the United States as the countries developed. My

117

knowledge of Canadian government today is very hazy–a pity.

*   *   *

Of course I received new books for Christmas, even though some of the givers know that I haven't read all the books I received or purchased last year; they know I want to read them all. I'm looking forward to reading Helen Hayes' memoir, *My Life in Three Acts*, published by Simon and Schuster, given to me by a daughter. Last year she gave me James Thom's *Long Knife*, based on the life of George Rogers Clark. My second daughter has kept me supplied with Pilcher's novels. I give her books about cats, and I give all our sons and daughters, whether they want them or not, some of my old books which I hope they'll like.

A train, going very fast, whistles, and I think of lines from a poem: "There isn't a train I wouldn't take, no matter where it's going." I can understand such an expression. Scenery I enjoy most is along roads that are new to me. Cities I would most like to visit are cities I have never seen. I enjoy very much going to a restaurant I have never before entered. I can understand people who have an inclination for adventure, but I have no yearning to travel in outer space! I don't even want to go hang gliding.

When our oldest son was very small, a little past toddler stage, he would have liked to go visiting in every house we passed while out walking. I can understand his being curious and his interest in people which continues today. I, too, am often curious about people and I'm very interested in meeting strangers, so how can I justify the fact that I have never greeted or talked with all of the people who live on our city block, probably no more than sixteen or eighteen families?

Air conditioning induces people to close doors and drapes and closed doors seem forbidding. It's been a long time since someone wrote, "I want to live in a house by the side of the road and be a friend to man."

     *   *   *

An article in *Newsweek* caused me to send a letter to the editor. I wanted to defend Dr. Benjamin Spock and people of my age who are classed as parents of baby boomers. What we learned from Dr. Spock's books caused us to rear children whose characters are flawed, according to the article. This is part of my letter. "Before Dr. Spock, parents were told they must never, never feed or pick up a crying baby if the time isn't right. The schedule must be followed. I was told by a mother who believed this, that she had stood over her baby's crib with her fists clenched so that she wouldn't break the pre-Spock era rules by picking up her crying child too soon . . . I welcomed Dr. Spock's advice and followed it . . . I do not believe they [our five children] would have been better off if they had been treated more rigidly."

*   *   *

It seems that pacifists can be a bit belligerent at times. Perhaps that's a good thing?

*   *   *

Our house was built in 1949. Without doubt, a few entryways for ants have come into being. At the moment, there are no ants in the kitchen, although some tried desperately to take part in our Christmas celebration. However, there are a few stragglers in the bathroom and they seem to have a preference for eating soap. I haven't determined whether they die after tasting the sweet-smelling deodorant soap, or whether they survive to come back for more. Soap-eating ants are an indication of some sort of statement about our culture, but I'm not sure what it is.

◁ February 4, 1993 ▷

I have read with interest *"Our American Cousin,"* the play Abraham Lincoln attended the night he was assassinated. (It's in Volume Five of the *West Virginia Heritage* series.) As I read I hoped that the president was relaxed enough when he saw the play to enjoy some of the funny lines. (I've probably misused the word "hope" here, but I hope readers will know what I mean.)

*   *   *

My long-lost first scrapbook has been found. It was hidden under some papers in a section of a trunk which I thought contained chiefly bank records. I began pasting clippings in a composition book, according to the first dated clipping, in 1931, and continued using that book until August, 1937. I am surprised to find a 1932 article which quotes from statements made by Louisa M. Alcott for the *Ladies' Home Journal.* The author of *Little Women* was born in 1832 and that fact lends interest to remarks she made about women. Her books tell us that she knew the importance of women. My clipping tells us that she said that women are asked to lead quiet, self-sacrificing lives, but they must have work for the mind. Many ways are open for women to learn, be and do much if they have the will and opportunity, she said, and women have the right to any branch of labor for which they prove their fitness. She expressed these thoughts sometime before 1888. She modified her statements by saying that these opinions should not be preached in the "rampant Women's Rights fashion," but by showing how much women can do by influencing home life.

*   *   *

I found *deniability* in a 1991 dictionary, but not in a 1979 listing. Is this a recently coined word convenient for use in some branches of government? What kind of actions can be performed with deniability by what kind of officials?

*   *   *

Jackson Stover knew the people of the Coal River area whom Jack E. Weller wrote about in *Yesterday's People.* He heard their version of the making of the slate road which crumbled when it rained. In response to my comments and questions about Mr. Weller's book, Mr. Stover had this–among other things–to say: "No doubt he has touched some psychological facets of the hill man's character. I am a hill boy and my people have been for generations. To give a correct appraisal, in my opinion, the writer would have to be one out of the hills who learned how to set down his innermost feelings, to write of his loves and hates, his faith and patriotism, his love of freedom and independence, his loyalties and devotion to duty, his abhorrence of sham and pretense."

Mr. Stover taught history for many years. He said that he could not accept a lot of Mr. Weller's ideas. He said that Jack Weller "overlooks the spirit that made America, [as exemplified by] the men whose love for freedom and independence led them into mountains and kept them in their fastness."

*　　　　*　　　　*

A discussion about apples reminded me that J. Stover gave me valuable information about apple orchards in West Virginia as he remembered them. More about apples later, perhaps.

❧ February 11, 1993 ☙

A discussion in a time of crisis, among people not very well acquainted, turned to a safe subject–apples. Delight with certain available grocery store apples was mentioned and recollections of apples eaten in the past. After a few minutes it was obvious that names of apples were not well-known by people discussing their merits. We didn't even recall the names of apples produced in the commercial orchards in our state–Red Delicious, York, etc.

As we talked, I recalled that Jackson Stover provided me with valuable information to help with articles about apples. In addition, for an article published in 1952, I interviewed people in the Charleston area and heard the names Early June, Ben Davis and Grimes Golden. I was told that one of the sweetest apples in the area at the beginning of the century was called the Sunday Sweet.

Other names I was given included Roman Beauty, Maiden Blush and Sheep Nose.

Mr. Stover recalled names from mountain-top farms that included apple orchards. Several such farms were located in the Cabin Creek–Paint Creek–Fulton Creek area. Each farm probably had twelve fruit trees, but some had as many as fifty. Mr. Stover remembered the names of Bird Egg or Little Early Striped apples, June apples, Transparents, Red Milams, White Milams, Winter apples and an apple called the Paremim. He mentioned that the Paremim was a red apple, grown in each of the orchards he knew, and his favorite. He had never seen the word in print and wasn't sure of the spelling when he gave me the apple information. *The New Columbia Encyclopedia* says *pearmain* is the name of several varieties of red apples and that the name is related to the word *parmayn* which refers to a variety of pear.) [See correction, p. 125]

Fruit trees on early homestead farms provided cider, vinegar, apple jelly, applesauce and apple butter. Sometimes apples were dried or stored in the ground like potatoes. Since apple trees may live as long as a hundred years, remnants of old orchards may be found in locations where you don't expect to find them. Remnants of old mountain-top orchards could be found "in the early 1920's and provided a choice find for the fellows who made use of the fruit to manufacture brandy along with 'White Mule'," according to Mr. Stover. Many of the orchards had been abandoned because families went down into the valleys when coal mines were opened.

Many people can recall a good-tasting apple, a favorite tree. We are fortunate that even in our West Virginia cities we have space for apple trees. Some are seedlings which are not always well-nourished, and may not last very long, but provide fruit which we can enjoy for a few seasons, even if we don't have a name for the variety. Where I lived from the year I was nine until I was twenty-two, in a coal community called Acme, located on Cabin Creek, we had in our small yard an apple tree which produced a large pale green, tart apple, name unknown. I often wondered if the house we lived in had once been a farmer's, long before the mines were opened. The apples were delicious.

⚞ February 18, 1993 ⚟

I see by the papers, as Will Rogers used to say–I think he's the one–that the North Fork of the Cranberry River has received a winter stocking of trout for the first time in 20 years. I caught a fish in the Cranberry River once, in the summer of 1937 or 38, the first fish I ever caught. I've caught very few since then, and actually I didn't really *catch* that one. A friend and I got up early to go fishing before others in our group were stirring. We tried, earnestly, to catch some fish, but failed while we were trying. Tired and ready to quit trying, I let my line dangle in the water while we were preparing to go look for breakfast. Suddenly a fish was on my line. Scared me to death, but I could say boastfully that I caught a fish. Since then, most of the fishing trips I've participated in included my sitting on the bank reading. (Wouldn't you know it?) 1938 was a long time ago, and, through the years, when I attempted to tell my fish story, I sometimes wondered if I confused the name Cranberry River with that of Cherry River. Actually, I'm still wondering. Maps don't help me a great deal. I recall that we reached the river by turning off from the highway at a spot approximately four miles from Craigsville. Whatever the location, I do remember accurately how I felt when I caught my first fish.

One of our daughters, a faithful *Scribbling* reader, says she prefers columns that discuss something at length, rather than those dealing with several subjects. I like to "throw out a thought," hoping readers will add their own thoughts or questions.

*　　　　　*　　　　　*

As our children grew, we often pointed out that most disagreements have two sides worth considering. Perhaps, grown-up, these adult children think that always trying to see two sides makes them "wishy-washy." I recall a quotation from long ago which I considered important. Someone said that we should beware having an open mind lest it become a yawning chasm. In 1974 an article I wrote was published under the title "Is My Mind A Yawning Chasm?"* I began the article by discussing the difficulties of being an arbitrator which seems, quite often, to be the role of a mother. I also mentioned that there are drawbacks to having the ability to see both sides of a problem. I wrote, "Sympathy, understanding, broadmindedness, empathy are great, but where do we stand? More to the point, where do we walk?" I still think it's important to see and try to understand the other fellow's viewpoint.

*　　　　　*　　　　　*

Reader's Digest Encyclopedic Dictionary, not the *New Columbia Encyclopedia*, is the source of the information I offered about pearmain apples.

*　　　　　*　　　　　*

Worth thinking about? "Be discontented with the world. But be respectful at the same time."–Chaim Potok in *Davita's Harp*, published by Fawcett Crest, 1985

*Perspectives, State Magazine *Gazette-Mail*, Charleston.

125

Mention coal, coal miners or coal communities and some listeners think only of strikes, disasters and grime produced by coal dust. I have pleasant memories of life in a coal community. My father was not an executive, not a "big boss." We did not live in one of the big houses on a hill. When I was nine we moved into a four-room house that had a bathroom behind the kitchen. (The bathtub had a broken leg.) Soon after we moved in, two rooms were added. They had been promised if my father would come to work as an electrician for that particular company.

The addition took up most of the front yard, but a space between the yard and the railroad provided a place to play baseball or Pretty Girls' Station and it served as a base for Hide and Seek and Red Rover. My brother and I played for hours with neighborhood children. Once we fastened a temporary homemade tent to the back porch and produced a circus. Five or six of our neighbors joined us in a pre-circus parade through the community: Our grandmother popped corn which she put in small paper bags that someone gave us. A large "crawdab" was one of the circus animals.

The back yard extended up the hill beyond the space for vegetables. Chickens were raised there, but later my brother and I made a miniature golf course in the chicken lot space. We played a few golf games with ten cent store clubs, but the most fun came from building the course, using cast-off odds and ends. Our mother found space for many flowers, including roses, hollyhocks and honeysuckle. The honeysuckle covered the small back porch and the coal house. We were lucky. We knew it was possible to have fun in a coal camp. Occasionally we climbed the hills to find a safe spot for a picnic. A few times we played Indians and settlers, perhaps in a spot not so safe. Once I found mayapple blossoms not far from our house. We found a place for winter sledding.

Schools and churches presented programs and plays. I remember a pie supper, being in plays and seeing my father in a play. We could travel a few miles to go to a carnival or Chautauqua presentation, a few miles in another direction to go swimming and two miles in a third direction to see a movie. We didn't always have a car, but during some of the years trains, and later, buses, were available.

Sitting on the small front porch on cool summer evenings was pleasant. Getting warm at the open fireplace in the winter was satisfying. Going to the large company store/post office building was a diversion. Sitting near the radio to hear Amos and Andy, Lowell Thomas or the Lucky Strike orchestra was entertaining. Playing cards or checkers was fun. Reading—even reading the same book seven times was a pleasure. And in the summer the large pale green apples grew on the tree in the tiny front yard. As children, we were not troubled by the sound of the huge coal cars jolting to a stop on the side track in front of the house. Life, usually, was good.

*   *   *

Panther Creek in the February 11th column was supposed to be Paint Creek.

ঝ March 4, 1993 ঙ

As I began to work on this week's column, I realized that only one thought which I considered as Scribbling material has come to mind. This thought was prompted by a visit to my favorite restaurant for lunch. I watched a recently hired waitress pick up drinking glasses as she cleared a table and it occurred to me that a point I mentioned in one of my earlier columns has not had far-reaching, long-lasting, world-shaking results. At least one reader may recall that I once wrote about the importance of picking up glasses near the bottom, as opposed to picking them up by the tops. Nit-picking? Of course, it is, and I could be accused of being on a route that leads to a state similar to that of Howard Hughes who, so we're told, became a germ fanatic, miserably. Yet, my eighth-grade home-economics teacher gave us very specific instructions in such matters. (Our grandchildren could relate emphatically their thoughts about my saying so often, "Did you wash your hands?" I'm fairly certain that they have definite opinions about this part of their daily lives, no ambivalence here).

How could anyone dare mention washing hands or picking up glasses in a certain way when thousands of people–millions, perhaps–live in misery, most of them living in conditions not of their own choosing? I remember, however, that someone has said that we should keep the little integrities and the big ones will be there when we need them. It would be very easy for me to quit, give up, be quiet. There is so much hurt, hatred, unfairness, squalor and plain old filth in the world that it can lead to a "What's the use?" attitude. It's tempting; we get tired. I'm not talking about sanitation now. Wasn't it Abraham Lincoln who made a special trip to return a few pennies given to him by mistake? He was keeping a "little integrity" and has since been admired for exhibiting the big integrities–fairness, honesty, steadfastness–as they relate to issues much bigger than a few pennies.

     *   *   *

128

Larry Gibson of Red House, West Virginia, is a descendant of one of the early "mountain-top homestead farm" families of Kanawha County. His great-grandfather, Jack Stanley, lived on Kayford Mountain and his is one of the farms Jack Stover remembered when he gave me information about apple orchards. Mr. Gibson, who is working to help establish a park on land his family owns, says that remnants of an early apple orchard still exist on the family's mountain-top property.

    *   *   *

Thinking of the value of considering both sides of arguments, I recalled that my philosophy of education classes seemed to emphasize the point that teachers should not inflict on students their opinions about such subjects as religion or politics, but should simply lead students to form their own opinions. I also remember hearing someone criticize this view, saying "That's the trouble with that school; they never tell you what to think." A related thought is expressed in "*Chutzpah*," a book by Alan Dershowitz, when he says, "A teacher has the right to be protected for espousing even idiotic views." I suppose what one does with espousal makes a difference.

◁ March 11, 1993 ▷

A close friend recently remarked that I enjoy everything. Actually, there are some things I don't enjoy. I don't like boxing matches or wrestling; I don't like football and what it does to people. I don't enjoy violent quarrels or fights or bickering, although I don't mind keeping up my end of a peaceful argument. I suppose one thing that prompted my friend to mention my enjoyment is the fact that I enjoy eating. Perhaps she was thinking of the fact that I enjoy people; I am always curious about people–their opinions, their interest, their reactions. If I should have to go to a football or baseball game, I could enjoy watching the spectators.

A few years ago–a few, compared to my age–I spent part of an evening in one of the upper stories of the World Trade Center Building in New York. I was the guest of friends who live and work in New York City and we went to a restaurant or club located in the building. I don't know whether we were on the 110th floor, but I didn't yearn to be any higher. I enjoyed the novelty of the experience, but I didn't relish being in the upper part of an unusually tall structure which could be hit by an airplane or damaged by an explosion such as that which occurred in the building February 26th. For that matter, I don't want to spend very much time in any of Charleston's glass-walled high-risers. Descending from a tall building in Columbus by means of a glass-fronted elevator attached to the outside of the building is an experience I'm not eager to repeat. (I recall being told that the elevator is not used when winds are high.) I don't know why we have to build skyscrapers when there is yet so much unoccupied space in our country, even in the state of New York.

*   *   *

During the fifties and sixties children in our house or yard could be seen scurrying to gain a vantage point for watching whatever motor or machine they heard approaching. I recall that they liked to watch trains, cement mixers, road scrapers, railroad work crews and trash collectors. I have noticed no such interest in recent years. Children do not get excited when trucks roll by on railroad tracks nor are they interested in the very unusual railroad repair machines. They may look up when a helicopter passes overhead if it's closer than usual. They look at balloons that appear on special occasions.

We had a television set in 1956, but it didn't eradicate interest in machines that appeared in our neighborhood. Something has caused a difference today; I see no evidence of interest in earthbound machines. What appears on television today must seem far more captivating, and perhaps, in a certain sense, more of a reality, than what passes by our house. I recall that our whole family was alerted when one of the first diesel engines was approaching and we watched and listened with neighbors as the new engine roared by. When I was young I was fascinated by the singing of work crews as they repaired railroads. I also longed to see inside of a caboose, but of course, I didn't get to do that until I became an adult and happened to attend a coal machinery exhibit where a caboose was open for inspection. I enjoyed that. To give today's young people credit for not being bored all the time: They do show interest in squirrels, rabbits, chipmunks and the giant woodpecker that sometimes appears in our yard.

◈ March 18, 1993 ◈

I am delighted to have found, in a wonderful old book published in 1902, the following tongue-in-cheek speech made by a young woman: "You've done a monologue . . . and I listened, as becomes inferior and subordinate woman." The words were spoken as part of the quick, light-hearted repartee between two young people on vacation from their work as newspaper reporters. The book, which I first read years ago and decided to reread while ignoring waiting household tasks, is *Lavender and Old Lace*, written by Myrtle Reed. I bought this copy in a second-hand bookstore in New York June 9, 1943, but I think I had read it somewhere long before that date. I have given the book to one of my daughters, but couldn't resist the temptation to read it again, escaping into thoughts of mystery hidden away in attic trunks, a lantern placed in a window at night and blossoming and resurrected romances.

*   *   *

A discussion of terrorism mentions murdering strangers for political reasons and asks if a sane person could do such a thing. But, isn't this what we do sometimes when we wage war, declared or covert? And, don't many people consider such wars justifiable? Perhaps I had better read (again?) *Arsenic and Old Lace*, published in 1941, compare it with *Lavender and Old Lace*, ruminate on the progress of civilization.

*   *   *

How can squirrels bury nuts so that most observers can't see where a hole has been dug and a nut buried? I've gone immediately to spots where I've seen squirrels hide nuts and couldn't see any evidence of ground disturbance. My husband roamed the woods in Kentucky as a boy, hunting and trapping, and later hunted in West Virginia, but I don't think he could walk into our yard and indicate where nuts are hidden. How do the squirrels find them, months after they've been buried? Another question: Do birds see or hear something that helps them locate worms? I'd really like to know. These questions and watching two playful squirrels on our front lawn help relieve my mind, diverting my thoughts from a consideration of what the United Nations has done, is doing and should do which was discussed with graphic illustrations on television a few minutes ago.

*   *   *

As I've mentioned before, I'm not overly fond of machines. Sometimes I disregard completely my electric mixer and mix by hand. Not long ago I bought a whisk for the first time and I've enjoyed using it for meringue and puddings. (A whisk, you may know, is not mechanical, but one has to whisk it by hand and arm power.) There is, however, one modern invention which I do enjoy using–the telephone. Yesterday I talked with someone I haven't seen since 1978, someone I first met by telephone when people at *Hillbilly* asked me to help her find Richwood after she reached Charleston, having come from New York City. It turned out that she couldn't make that trip, but she came to Charleston later and we've exchanged pleasant visits. Today I spoke, by telephone, with my aunt who is 91 and many miles away; I had an opportunity to tell her, perhaps for the last time, that I love her. I do like telephones.

◁ March 25, 1993 ▷

Astonishing facts: Snow fell in June, July and August in The United States during the year following the 1815 eruption of a volcano in Indonesia. Today approximately 500 million people are living near active volcanoes at various locations throughout the world. (Information gleaned from *The National Geographic*.)

*   *   *

Somehow, looking at the narrow shoveled pathway leading from our door to the street, with snow banked high on either side, and then seeing a slight-figured jogger going by, bending forward a little, inclined toward the icy pavement, makes me think of evolution. I'm not sure of the connection between that word and the two observations. Perhaps there isn't any, and probably the word *resolution* is more closely connected to the two sights. One could say that this paragraph of scribbling is a waste of space. I'll blame it on the snowstorm. Is it really the storm of the century? Somehow I'm skeptical about that classification. I daresay there are people in the Webster Springs-Richwood area who could provide descriptions of snowstorms that would dwarf what we've had this year. And what about the people who live on prairies and in locations similar to that mentioned by Walt Thayer in his letter to *Hillbilly*? They know a great deal about storms, many of which happened long before we had television meteorologists. I'm not implying that Mr. Thayer lived before we had television; I don't know how old he is. I'm simply referring to his description of snow and ice which caused his injury last year. He lives in the state of Washington at present. I recall reading of people being lost in wide-open country in snowstorms, in places where there were no mountains to bump into. I think that would be quite frightening. I've read of children trying to find their way home in snowstorms, in the days before school buses were invented. Perhaps sometimes they rode horses which helped them reach home. I asked my husband, who grew up on a Kentucky mountain-top farm, whether he was ever lost in a snowstorm. He said that he hadn't been lost in snow, but he was lost once in a rainstorm, after he moved to West Virginia. He had gone hunting, going up the mountain from Dawes Hollow on Cabin Creek. The fog got so thick that he couldn't see the mountain tops; he realized that the stream was flowing the wrong way, and he managed to go back the way he had come. Leaves were still on the trees and he had broken some limbs which helped him find his way. Today I've learned that the United States weather service was established in 1870 and that Aristotle wrote about studying the weather long before that. Also, I may be able to spell meteorology without using the dictionary if I should ever have occasion to use the word again. So much for progress. Still on the subject of snow: A quick look at the television screen lets me see men lying in snow firing deadly-looking weapons, aimed at someone, somewhere in the world. What more can I say?

After I mentioned in last week's column the possibility that people of the Webster Springs-Richwood area could tell tales of blizzards in their area that would rival any of this year's experiences, I recalled Hobert Skidmore's description of snow in his novel, *O Careless Love*. This Webster Springs native put a character in his book who remembered what happened when the snow was "tail deep to a standing deer." That is a rather unusual way to measure a snowfall, and not exactly scientific, but it probably seemed an apt description to people in the past. This particular one of Hobert's novels is set in 1923.

One of the most graphic, moving descriptions of the difficulties experienced in trying to get a paper out in cold weather may be found in the novel written by Georgia Heaster about Anne Royall, one of the earliest women journalists. Ms. Heaster's story is undoubtedly the product of research and some of the details in her book may be confirmed by reading Anne Royall's journal, first printed in 1826 and reprinted in 1970. Ms. Heaster's book was serialized in *Hill and Valley* magazine, Volumes Five and Six, and copies of the magazine may be found in the West Virginia Archives Library (also in WVU Library and Brown University Library.)

In Chapter 22 of the novel *Devilish Angel* we are told that it is so cold in Washington, D.C., that the Potomac is frozen over entirely and the city is buried in white. Anne Royall has been producing a newspaper called *The Huntress*. Her newspaper shop and living quarters are in the same building and she divides her supply of wood between the two sections. Although she has hung quilts around the walls to keep out the wind and snow, the wind came in through the cracks. Snow must be swept off the press and bricks heated to try to thaw the frozen printing machine. When the press finally begins to "groan and move," there is something wrong and Anne takes the machine apart to find the trouble and get it working again. Then, because the press is too cold and the newsprint is thin and of poor quality, the paper sticks to the roller and comes off in pieces. In spite of this, Anne finally goes out to deliver "a few sorry copies." She is ready to give up when she delivers a complimentary copy of her paper to *The Globe* office. There she is given money to buy a pair of shoes and told that she will be supplied with newsprint because her non-partisan newspaper is providing a service to the country.

A note from *Hillbilly* reader Walt Thayer says that on March 11, daffodils and crocuses were in bloom in his area. He lives in the state of Washington. The snow is almost all gone here in Charleston (W.Va.), but during my trip downtown today, March 22, I learn that memories and talk of the blizzard have not melted. A woman on the bus says that she still thinks the storm of 1978 was worse, and the girl who cuts my hair says that her family in Beirut called to know if she survived the storm which was publicized in their city.

Overheard in the salon: "It's just like everything else–the same thing every day." The speaker had mentioned spending time in Florida. It seems to me that wide differences exist between "the same things every day" as experienced by different people. Some people, no doubt, would be glad to exchange their sameness for someone else's.

⚜ April 8, 1993 ⚜

If a man plants shade trees when he knows he won't be around when they are full-grown, then he has begun to discover the meaning of human life, according to Elton Trueblood, as quoted in *The Fountain*, March 24.

    *   *   *

A letter from a *Hillbilly* subscriber postmarked March 16, reached my mailbox March 22. Our snowstorm (blizzards) may have had something to do with the delay. The letter came from Mr. Thayer in the state of Washington, which he says is Big Apple Country. He wrote the letter March 16 and said he had just received his February 11 and March 11 issues of *Hillbilly*, and decided to tell me of apples which he remembers from his early years, including Wealthy, Wolf River, Duchess and Spitzenberg. He says the pale green apple which I remember may have been the Eastern Greening. Mr. Thayer has been in the Northwestern United States since 1936, he says, and he is able to provide a wealth of information about apples grown in that area today.

    *   *   *

A long time ago, when all of our children were very young, I worried about hunger and about apples going to waste. I wrote a great many words about apples in America. The words could be called a poem; some of them even rhymed. I wrote about older people gleaning apples along the roadside, about suburban apples being raked up and discarded, about undiscovered apples growing in lost orchards. I asked why we couldn't gather the apples, send them across the sea to hungry children. I wrote those words in the days before we were assailed with pictures of starving people, and before national efforts to help were widely publicized. In the closing lines I decried myself as an impractical idealist, accused of having applesauce running

137

out of my ears! (It was supposed to be a slightly funny poem.)

I still regret the fact that all apples aren't salvaged, and worry about wasted food. Today I discarded something that could have been eaten before it was too old, but it was not needed or wanted when it was edible. With all of our know-how, why can't we manage so that people do not go hungry while some of us have more than we need? I know–I'm only a little old lady in flat-heeled shoes, but somehow there should be a way.

*   *   *

Again this year I've been given the honor and the task of critiquing plays written by high school students. I've read only a few pages, but I've found that terms I'm not familiar with have been added to today's teenagers' vocabulary. Today I've learned the definition of *grifter*; it may not be a new word, but I didn't know about it previously; I've heard the word *dork* before, perhaps spoken by a grandchild, but it's not in my dictionary. Incidentally, I asked our junior high grandchildren if they know the difference between *you're* and *your*. I am pleased to find they do. Perhaps some computers are better than others?

❧ April 15, 1993 ☙

Breathes there a woman who hasn't dreamed of being saluted with a courtly bow–the old-fashioned kind of greeting? The vision probably included a hat with a feather on it, a very long feather, and there may have been a white horse somewhere in the background of the fantasy. Sooner or later, we learn that courtly bows are rare, and that flowery speeches of praise and endearment may be missing from every-day events. Actually, I think I prefer the

138

absence of honeyed words and I have found that sometimes silence is golden.

For example, there was the time early in my married life when it seemed to be my fault that my husband's brand new, as yet untried fishing rod disappeared in the muddy waters of a swollen river, never to be seen again, unless someone discovered it years later. It seemed to me that it was hours and hours before my husband spoke to me. Of course, he was very busy trying to control the boat part of the time, but when he finally said something, I had begun to wonder if he would ever talk to me again, although I realized very well that silence was preferable to speeches he might have made . . .

. . . Honestly, loyalty and respect for a spouse seem to be more important than constant flattery and regular use of sugar-sweet expressions . . . If this were the age of courtly bows, I might have to be constantly curtsying, and I might have to practice blushing and hiding behind a fan if I were constantly flattered. Worst of all, I might begin to doubt that the flatterer really meant what he was saying.

*   *   *

An article in a recent issue of *Newsweek* includes the information that children as young as seven, eight or ten years old have tried to commit suicide. In the same issue of the magazine Malcolm Jones, Jr. said that in 1991 eight out of ten Americans said they expect to answer for their sins on Judgment Day. If that is an accurate figure, representing honest answers, it might be very interesting to compare those figures with figures showing the percentage of our population accused of committing crimes.

*   *   *

Perhaps if I see the following statement in print, I will fully realize that the words tell of something that has actually happened: I have copy-edited my long-thought-about novel, signed a royalty contract and checked the first set of proofs.

*   *   *

I firmly believe that writing is for everyone, no matter if you have never written before, or if it has been fifty years, more or less, since your doctoral thesis was published. I'm speaking of all kinds of writing–for amusement, for sharing with friends, for club meetings, in letters or journals. Someone said that writing helps you clarify your thoughts. That could be very valuable.

∂ April 22, 1993 ∂

A paper published in Virginia announced that Radford University will begin offering a program of Peace and World Security Studies. The paper, *New River Free Press*, reports that approximately 250 U.S. colleges and universities offer programs concerning peace-related issues such as arms control, global security and conflict resolution. A long time ago I was enrolled in a class offered by Marshall College titled "The History of American Diplomacy." We had two weighty texts; one consisted of copies of treaties and letters, instructions of Congress and other documents. One book was published in 1947; the other, in 1948. Perhaps I'll look at them again someday to see if I can understand why diplomacy hasn't been more effective in keeping us out of war. Chiefly, now, what I remember about the class (I think my grade was a B) is that on one night when I had read the assignment in only one of the two texts we had a surprise quiz on the material I hadn't read. Needless to say, my grade was not a B on that pop quiz. Meanwhile, I can hope that the 250 peace-related courses will help some of our young people further the cause of peace in the world.

*   *   *

One of our Charleston newspapers reports that no Pulitzer Prize has been awarded this year for editorial writing and adds the additional information that this is the seventh time that no prize has been awarded for editorial writing. This seems to emphasize the fact that today's problems are overwhelming and sometimes leave editors speechless.

*   *   *

Meanwhile, today, in my kitchen, I "lit a small candle." I didn't really burn anything; I'm referring to the fact that I cleaned the outside surface of our refrigerator, the easily visible part which definitely needed cleaning. Better to clean a little than not at all. Right? And some small effort toward peace-keeping is better than none at all.

*   *   *

Outside, the sun has been highlighting the yellow and orange tulips and the beautiful pansies which one of our daughters gave us. They have been carefully planted by my husband and provide a pleasant sight for him to look at while he rests momentarily from his task of chopping and preparing to remove a huge tree stump. The stump is there because we lost one of our trees to termites. Speaking of bugs, the ants have given up trying to establish a colony inside our house, perhaps because we followed the advice of a *Hillbilly* reader who recommended the use of boric acid powder to discourage their invasion. Incidentally, a news article published in *The Charleston Gazette* March 23, reminded readers that large quantities of boric acid are dangerous to children and animals, so the product should be used carefully.

And I must proceed to work on our Income Tax report which I have delayed doing, a fault which I have criticized in others.

I'm beginning this scribbling later in the week than usual. I've been working too steadily at the task of gathering information and typing names and addresses on 1,000 labels. While doing so, I've ignored signals I've received telling me that I should cease and desist–in other words, take time to rest a little. The wonderful inner mechanisms we human beings are provided with try very hard to warn us when we need rest, but sometimes, being stubborn individuals, we ignore such warnings.

I've felt compelled to work at this current task with few intervals of rest because I'm pulling names from several sources and I have to try to realize whether I'm duplicating. Although an address book and three sets of cards are alphabetized (for the most part), other lists, such as names of people attending workshops, are not in alphabetical order. Being more inclined to read fiction than to study scientific manuals, and not owning a machine that would do the work for me, I can't think of a way that I could have simplified and shortened the task. However, the goal is in sight; when I type names on approximately 119 more labels I will have finished 1,000.

*   *   *

Yesterday, during a short break, I picked up a notebook that included comments I wrote in 1964 and 1965 concerning certain problems related to adjusting to the new social conditions of that time period. As I read, I realized that we, as a nation, as human beings, have made progress in spite of the fact that current happenings in the world are overwhelming and frightening.

*   *   *

Sometime in the fifth or sixth century Theognis, whoever he was, said, "Be not too zealous; moderation is best in all things." I think that's debatable, but I admit I should try to act wisely when I need rest. As I thought about this, I recalled a time, years ago, when I was given such a warning. We were on the first day of our vacation and had traveled many miles. I hadn't been typing labels before we left home, but as I often did when the children were small and clothes had to be ironed, I had probably stayed up all night packing suitcases. Actually my own inner consciousness yelled, "Whoa! It's time to get some rest." I was surprised, but I heeded the warning and so have survived and reached the day of wash and wear, no ironing needed.

Considering the 1,000 labels task, I suppose I could have made a separate list for each letter of the alphabet and listed all the names before transferring them to labels. Once, I might have done so, to be sure I didn't have duplicates. Now, callously, I say, "A few extra postage stamps probably won't be too greatly cost-prohibitive." So it goes. Theognis may have had the right idea. Probably I should think about that, after I have a little more rest.

❧ May 6, 1993 ❧

A pleasant visit in a pleasant home set me thinking about the differences in houses, their furnishings and their owners. I had met and talked with the congenial hostess only once before, but during that first contact it took us only a few minutes to discover that both of us had read and enjoyed Rosamunde Pilcher's books, and that both of us had discovered and read a similar book called *The Pink Bus* or *The Lavender Bus*, or some such, which has a setting similar to Pilcher's books.

The home in which a friend and I enjoyed being guests for lunch is filled with objects which the owner has made, discovered, rejuvenated or cherished as family treasures. It takes only a few minutes to realize that objects in the house–decorations and furniture–are enjoyed by the owner, the hostess. Remember when people made little rosettes by gathering and sewing into a puff or pocket round pieces of cloth? These were then used for pillow tops or, perhaps, for small coverlets, or as I observed today, as a protective cover for the back of an upholstered chair. A beautiful framed picture and a lovely clock have been rescued from basement hiding places.

In my opinion these help make an important contrast to homes we might see elsewhere, filled with the most elegant expensive furniture placed in rooms that are devoid of any homelike atmosphere. Of course, I realize that people who know me and have seen my dusty, overly cluttered house may have very definite criticisms of what they see here, but usually they've been too kind to tell me. I would like to be rid of some of my scars and scratches, and it would be nice if I polished and waxed more often, but I simply can't imagine living without books and papers, and I'll always like the sketches, paintings and wood carvings members of the family have contributed to our unplanned interior decorating.

*   *   *

A young friend who lives in Canada made an interesting observation in a letter I received this week. Canadians, he said, tend to look outward, while the United States view is inward.

The news magazine that comes to our house each week, ordered by one of our daughters, sometimes has front-of-the-magazine articles and cover illustrations so upsetting that I sometimes start at the back of the magazine, saving the most disturbing news for the final look. This is cowardly, I suppose, and contrary to my once-declared philosophy of trying to make the best of things. (Or is it?) At any rate, I found what I consider a good point expressed on page 74 of the May 10th *Newsweek*. Meg Greenfield says in her last-page article that we should try to modify our tendency to rate presidents, past and present, as either all bad or all good. She says that we wouldn't rate our friends or family members this way. Perhaps we wouldn't, but it is easy for us to let faults we perceive loom large in our thinking about people.

Not having thought of anything interesting to say about the squirrel and the giant woodpecker that acknowledged each other's presence yesterday in our back yard, I turned to some old clippings of a column I wrote for a weekly newspaper in the 1930's. In one of them I mentioned judging a person's degree of refinement, whatever that is, not by how he holds a fork, but by his "inward charm and grace, by his regard for the feelings of others, an amount of forgetfulness of self, the inclination and ability to look for and find the more worthwhile things— kindness, gentleness, cheerfulness, music, beauty."

Such a statement wouldn't be of much interest to the people in Bosnia today or to people in many other locations. Any such remarks would be drowned out by the sound of battle or the sound of mourning. Yet, it does seem that often tragedy causes people to be more considerate of

145

each other, and emergencies draw people together. Hobert Skidmore's books about men in World War II emphasized this fact and his writing about the war has been praised by people who knew what he was talking about. He wrote that although men had learned to fight and kill, "Learned it suddenly and meanly . . . somehow it had made them gentle." "They were all exhausted, but they were thoughtful and careful of one another."

World War II was different in many respects from any other war or non-wars that have occurred since 1946, and I wonder if Hobert Skidmore's thoughts about men at war would apply as readily to Korea or Vietnam or Desert Storm. Attitudes among civilians, those of us who stayed at home, were definitely not the same during these conflicts, probably with good reason. But who am I to say?

In one of my old 1930's columns I mentioned that someone whose opinion I respected had told me that my columns, called "Scribblings of a Cabin Creeker," were too long and tended to be boring. I don't remember who told me that. It may have been my father, but I doubt it. He would not have added the second part of the statement, even if he thought so.

     *   *   *

A statistic included in one of those old columns, drawn from a college notebook: At one time in [ancient] Rome there were 2300 places where bread was dispensed under police supervision.

☙ May 20, 1993 ❧

The letter from Canada which I mentioned recently contained clippings about a coal mining disaster which caused the death of 26 miners on May 9, 1992, in a Nova

Scotia mine. Reports in a Toronto paper concerning the current investigation of the disaster included statements similar to those we are accustomed to hearing in reports of investigations in the United States. I hadn't realized that there are coal mines in Canada. My one-volume encyclopedia tells me that minerals are important in Canada and several are mentioned, but not coal. It also says that one of Canada's problems is that some industries, including mining, are controlled by foreign interests, including companies in the United States. My *New Columbia Encyclopedia* was published in 1975 and conditions may have changed, but it is always surprising to discover how little we know about other countries.

The young Canadian who sent me the clippings is very much interested in coal mining history, especially that of West Virginia mining. In his response to some of my comments about Canada, he said that he considers Canada a true melting pot.

Speaking of acquiring surprising information, I was somewhat skeptical when a taxi driver told me a few years ago that there are salt mines under one or more of our Great Lakes. I have since been told that this is true.

*   *   *

It is heartening to see people flocking to places where flowers are for sale. I once wrote an essay in response to a statement made by someone who said courage and stamina may become extinct if we have no wars. It seems to me that the speaker was lacking in knowledge of the realities of life. Courage and stamina are required in daily life, over and over again. It takes courage and stamina to keep working at a job the worker dislikes. It takes stamina to keep cleaning and scrubbing when floors and entire houses continue to get dirty again. It takes courage and stamina to work in dangerous places, to care for sick people, to continue to work faithfully and well in many types of service positions.

People are exhibiting stamina when they buy, plant and care for flowers. When they try in any way to nurture beauty they are not succumbing to hopelessness. Countless people overcome physical handicaps and proceed to learn and care for themselves. Children exhibit courage when they are determined to act and learn as well as possible, in spite of the fact that they haven't clothes or resources similar to those of their schoolmates. Fathers and mothers exhibit stamina when they give up dreams of travel and home ownership and put the needs of their children first.

It takes courage to go to war, but there's a place for courage in a world without war. Courage is required to preserve ideals. Stamina is required daily. Courage is many-faceted.

◈ May 27, 1993 ◈

In our family we celebrate birthdays with birthday dinners. Anyone who lives near enough, and most of them do, is invited to come to dinner, or after dinner, for cake. We try to have ready the favorite foods of the birthday person, indulge in a bit of good-natured teasing about the birthday person's age, and express our wishes for happiness in the future.

I read somewhere once that people who make big fusses over birthdays have character flaws. I'm not sure that person was right. I suppose I have a slight complex about birthday gifts; I'm a bit fearful that I'll receive something I don't like and will be hard put to know how to say thank you effectively. I usually worry if I think someone has spent too much money, and I actually grieve a little when I receive a beautiful gift of clothing that doesn't fit. Most of the people in our family chain know me well enough to help me weather the birthday with integrity intact; they give me gifts like paper clips, pens, note cards, envelopes and sometimes books. These help me say thank you, most sincerely.

Speaking of birthdays, let's consider the beauty of gift wrapping paper. Quite often, at our house, we try to salvage the used paper, use it for the next birthday. What is sold for gift wrapping today is often a work of art; it's expensive, and should not be thrown away. However, what I've used for the May birthday has become quite skimpy; some of the packages I wrapped have unwrapped spaces on the bottom. I think I'll have to buy some paper before the July birthday dinner. However, if I haven't bought any new wrapping paper by that time, I'm not adverse to wrapping a gift in a newspaper or a brown paper sack. I still have some red ribbons stored in the old trunk where I keep some very important papers, including any salvaged birthday wrappings. The ribbon would help.

Thinking of writing these thoughts, I thought again of all the misery, sorrow, fear and suffering that exist elsewhere in the world. I thought, briefly, of writers and philosophers in the past who surely knew of such suffering, perhaps had experienced some of it, yet wrote of their hopes for the world. Perhaps, expressing hope is not useless.

Yesterday someone new in the neighborhood volunteered help with my husband's weed cutting. Today a worried secretary called concerning a daughter's hospital test. A short while later, I learned our daughter was safely back at her office desk. The robin diligently feeds her family perched on our fence. A squirrel hops through the yard and leaps over the neighbor's flower bed without harming the flowers. My husband carries our granddaughter's bicycle wheel to the car; he's off to look for materials or help with his mending. Returning home, he stops to pick up part of a bouquet of flowers; he wants to replace the wilted ones with more of the small white flowers he says were called fence roses when he was growing up on a farm. A few things are right with the world. Someday, perhaps, hope will be more prevalent, replacing despair.

❧ June 3, 1993 ☙

Most writers learn that fame and fortune don't come easily, if ever. The world is so full of words that one person's writing is something like a child's whisper in a crowd watching a stock car race. Although I've had one play staged and a small one published, others I have written keep traveling through the mail and coming back to me. However, a place for two of them was found recently when a Marshall University Library staff member asked for more of my writing about life in coal communities, and I sent two plays which will be placed in a collection of material available for research. Also, this month I received a request from Berea College asking for copies of two of my unpublished papers about the Skidmores. I was glad to comply because I can't quit hoping that all of the twins' books may be reprinted, and at my age I'm pleased to have my writing appear in archives, if not in view of the general public.

Here are some of the narrator's speeches in *This, Too, Is Heritage*, one of the plays I sent to Morrow Library:

" . . . We intend to present one or more facets of a shiny black diamond, a look beyond, and into, life in the small gray houses, nestled far below the turnpike, starting with a glimpse of history, progressing to the present. Plays about coal mining people have been few, and have made little stir in theater circles. Once upon a time Samuel French published a book of gloomy presentations about mining people, a volume titled *The Shadow of the Mine*. These plays resounded with the noise of houses being boarded up as towns were abandoned. They included the noise of bar-room brawling, the roar of explosions and the sound of women weeping. This was in the 1920's and the plays gave only a partial view of the people and the mining communities. Much later, Billy Edd Wheeler wrote a beautifully poetic play about a mining community, calling up pictures of the West Virginia community where he had lived when he was young. The play was exciting, but for one reason or another, *Slatefall* didn't get the attention that *The Hatfields and McCoys* received. Audiences, it seems, haven't wanted to hear about miners, or producers have thought they didn't . . .

"[One of] Leo Pride's play [s] . . . published in the Samuel French collection, reminds us of the rich addition to our country that occurred when people from Europe came to work in coal. They walked into the mines beside the native mountaineers, worked with them, and walked out in the evening into the narrow valleys where smoke curled from chimneys and families waited with bath water heating on the stove, supper cooking and children running to see if Daddy brought home a treat in his dinner pail.

" . . . The mother and daughter in the play talk of their life in the mining community and recall life in the old country. Now, the mother says, the lost family members no

151

longer lie on white pillows. They have been lost in the blackness of the mine, and the play ends on a tragic note.

"Tragedy is only part of the story, one facet of the shiny black diamond . . . "

❧ June 10, 1993 ❧

I'm guilty. I used the word *adverse* when *averse* would have been better. I mailed the column with the unwise choice of words four days ago. Suddenly, this morning, May 22, it occurred to me that I should consult my dictionary. I had the feeling that someone was thinking of my choice of words and wondering about it. When I was working on the column, the word *adverse* just popped into my mind and then out of the typewriter. I think that we often use words in writing that we don't use in ordinary every-day conversation. Letters written a hundred years ago often seem stately. Sometimes, reading old documents, I wonder if the writers were not better educated than we are today. Of course, Benjamin Franklin wouldn't know the meaning of *nanosecond, tropism, or megalev,* but neither do I.

*   *   *

One of our daughters says that she found extremely disturbing a magazine cover that pictured a child injured by warfare. Because she thought the picture important, she posted it on a bulletin board and was disappointed when someone removed it. She thinks it regrettable that people hide from the facts.

So often we feel hopeless and helpless and as a result do tend to bury our heads in the sand. Perhaps waxing indignant occasionally may have some effect. The following lines are part of something I wrote titled, *"Men*

Sitting at Mahogany Tables." (First published in *Grab-a-Nickel*):

What of men sitting at mahogany tables?
Do they never see faces of beautiful children?
Not the starving faces, the hopeless dull eyes–
We block our minds, shield our thoughts from these.
But faces with eyes open wide,
With laughing eyes, beautiful faces,
Faces in countries not ours . . .
But what of these men sitting at mahogany tables?
Do they never see
The faces of the children they plan to kill–
Children with beautiful faces, children in countries
not ours?

Although this was published in a much longer form, it has been criticized as being too didactic. But that's what happens when we try to tell people how we think things should be. Often, however, honest emotion is evident as in the following lines written by a teacher friend of mine five days after the Pearl Harbor attack in 1941. Helma Forsyth and I were very young at that time and rather timid about sharing our written thoughts, but she has given me permission to quote the following lines, part of her emotional poem:

What plan of life, What pattern.
May one hope to follow
In a world of war? Yet it is not I who suffer.
I know nothing of hunger,
Of death, of horrible destruction.
I know only fear–Fear of life devoid
Of home and love and children.
What madness to offer more of this to little ones.

*   *   *

153

A television program informs me that there are 25,000 restaurants in New York City and that dining out is a favorite pastime of New Yorkers. Interesting.

ॐ June 17, 1993 ॐ

Arguments in favor of and in opposition to construction of a proposed high voltage power line seem worth considering. Both proponents and opponents seem sincere. The democratic process often seems intolerably slow and inefficient, but it certainly seems preferable to dictatorship, and having help with making decisions should be a comfort to executives in business or government. It would be most difficult for one person in charge to have to decide all questions all the time. Perhaps such difficulty explains why rulers in the past sometimes resorted to saying, "Off with her head!" or "Put him in the stocks!" when problems seemed to have no easy solution.

It is often difficult to see problems clearly, and people may change their minds after having time for careful consideration. I was somewhat surprised to hear a remark made by a veteran planning to participate in a Memorial Day exercise. An elderly man, one of a group shown on TV, said he had once considered it very wrong when pacifists protested or went to Canada to avoid serving in the armed forces, but he had reconsidered and now he thinks that no one should fight.

As I thought of veterans, I recalled traveling during World War II, going to port cities where I would have an opportunity to spend a few hours with my sailor husband. I carried our marriage certificate in my luggage, because rumor had it that some hotels required proof of marriage. How times have changed!

I don't recall ever having to present proof of wedlock, but I do recall being chastised by a travel agent in Boston because I asked if the rooms were clean in a hotel he was recommending. He reminded me, indignantly, that I was not in Washington or New York, but in New England. We were lucky to find a vacant room of any sort at that time, but I had good reason to ask about cleanliness, having stayed in one hotel (not in Boston) that was definitely not in A-1 condition, and where no one in charge showed the least concern about marriage certificates. Boston's Hotel Vendome was clean and spacious, and waiters in the dining room were solicitous of elderly people who were permanent residents in the hotel. (Although I was not elderly at the time, the waiter for my table made sure I used my steak knife correctly.)

During World War II many people traveled who had not dreamed of traveling before and a spirit of friendliness and helpfulness pervaded. As in other wartime situations, young men who had never hoped to further their education received extensive training. A pilot, for example, might complete work at three colleges as part of his preparation for war. Perhaps, someday, similar opportunities for all will be available in peacetime.

Speaking of being chastised, an editor, a Californian, I think, wrote me a long, lecturing letter because I had begun a poem with a question. I was so astonished it was some time before I recalled Lowell's famous familiar question, "What is so rare as a day in June?"

*   *   *

Housecleaning, painting, moving furniture cause me to ask myself a question: Is it possible that I have more books and papers than I need?

Forming thread from growing plants and learning to put threads together in intricate patterns that hold their position and become garments–what a wonderful accomplishment! I sit resting, thinking, look down at the dress I am wearing and marvel at the fact that I can see the interweaving of threads making a design so small that we almost need a magnifying glass to learn that threads are woven together. I am amazed, thinking of the machinery required to do such weaving. Surely, learning to make cloth is a greater accomplishment than making an atomic bomb. Boris Pasternak wrote, ". . . what has for centuries raised man above the beast is not the cudgel but an inward music."

     *   *   *

Interest in writing is alive and well in West Virginia. In spite of the fact that the conference announcement was late, attendance at the annual WV Writer's Conference at Cedar Lakes June 4, 5, and 6 was good. Approximately 600 manuscripts were entered in the annual contest. Winners in the 11 categories represented Putnam, Cabell, Kanawha, Marion, Hancock, Monongalia, Wood, Wayne, Logan, Jackson, Gilmer, Boone, Greenbrier, Doddridge, Ohio, Jefferson, Calhoun, Brooke, Tucker and Pocahontas Counties.

Mountain State Press is also alive and well, with its three newest books selling well. This is an organization of great importance to West Virginia writers and readers, and it would not exist if Jim Comstock of Richwood, W. Va., had not seen the need for such a publishing house, formed to produce books by West Virginians or about West Virginia. Members of the first board of directors were chosen by *Hillbilly* readers, and the first organizational meeting was held in Richwood. The office for the press is now located at the University of Charleston, and requests for information about books available may be addressed to Mountain State Press in care of the university. (Zip code, 25304.)

*　　　　　　　*　　　　　　　*

Disappointment because something you have written is rejected can be overwhelming, but writers need to realize that judging has, unavoidably, a subjective element. An editor may decide to publish a certain manuscript on the day he receives it, and the next day change his mind. Another editor may decide to publish the submission. However, it is good to try to look objectively at what we have written and consider ourselves lucky if an editor or judge has commented specifically.

*　　　　　　　*　　　　　　　*

Pansies and other flowers in our yard are continuing to flourish and we've enjoyed lettuce and kale from the vegetable garden. Sad to say, but I enjoy the first early garden gleanings a little more than I enjoy the huge baskets of vegetables picked later in the season, quite often late Saturday afternoon, because–lazy, ungrateful person that I am–I know extra work is called for. We've discovered a good solution, however. We know that we can give some of the abundance to neighbors or others who will welcome it.

❧　July 1, 1993　❧

If road builders hadn't made superhighways, we could enjoy seeing more of towns along the road, but we wouldn't be able to reach so many far-flung places on short vacations. I think I'd almost opt for seeing more of the towns we bypass. Towns and cities and villages are *not* all alike. They have different flavors.

*　　　　　　　*　　　　　　　*

My aunt, who is now 91, says that when she was receiving nurse's training at the old Hansford Hospital (in the Kanawha Valley), the usual treatment for pneumonia was application of poultices held in place with a vest-like garment. In addition, the patient was given a shot of morphine. (It's easy to guess that members of the medical profession heartily welcomed the discovery of penicillin.) My aunt's father, my Grandfather Young, died of pneumonia which occurred after a fall from a coal car.

      *   *   *

Thought while traveling: Can you imagine what might happen in traffic if all rear view mirrors were suddenly removed from cars? Does anyone recall when such mirrors were first installed? I'm fairly certain that the first car our family had, a Star, I think, did not have a rear view mirror. That car had side curtains that had to be put up when it rained. (If the rain came as a surprise, the person putting up the curtains might be soaked because, as I recall, the curtains were attached by someone standing outside the car.) Another car we had, an Essex, may have had a rear view mirror, but I rather doubt it.

      *   *   *

It seems that in some parts of the country, including where I live, "How ya doin'?" has replaced "Hello" or "Hi" or even "Howdy." I don't know whether "How do you do?" is ever uttered anywhere hereabout these days. Perhaps the pendulum is swinging back toward "How do you do?" but I rather doubt it. At least, it is still safe in some areas to greet passersby, who may be strangers, saying "How ya doin'?" Hardly anyone ever answered the question "How do you do?," but it seems that people do reply to "How ya doin'?"

      *   *   *

Scanning a stack of newspapers after returning from vacation doesn't seem nearly as intriguing as reading a morning newspaper each day. Perhaps it's because daily news often makes us wonder if the world will exist tomorrow, and when we have several days' papers to look at, we know that we have escaped a few disasters. Then, too, we may feel a little guilty to be taking so much time with old newspapers. Reading one paper, drinking another cup of coffee, and even working one puzzle before starting to work can be excused, I think.

*   *   *

Journeying toward Mt. Airy, North Carolina, I tried to recall whether that town is the place my grandmother said her family left when they moved to Kentucky. We really should listen carefully to our elders, but when we're young, other things seem more important. A pity. So sayeth this scribbling grandmother.

❧ July 8, 1993 ❧

Red birds surely must know when the Fourth of July is near. They have no trouble at all deciding when to return to our yard and they promptly find and make good use of watermelon seeds placed where they can find them.

*   *   *

I've thought about it, but I'm not sure what my response should be when someone says, "You don't look any older than you did the first time I saw you." Sometimes the speaker may add, "I first met you a long time ago." In addition to not being sure what to say, I'm not sure what I should think about the speaker, the remark, or my appearance, now or in the past. But, since I've been told a time or two that I think too much, I won't spend much time trying to decide what my response should be.

*   *   *

I think I am the only person in our immediate family who doesn't like fireworks displays. I suppose I could blame my dislike on my mother's fearful cautioning when my brother and I were young–her warnings about getting an eye put out or fingers blown off, but there is more to my dislike than an inheritance of fear of accidents. The expensive, spectacular explosions intended for entertainment remind me too vividly of the destruction that occurs when other "fireworks," such as million dollar missiles, are exploded for purposes other than entertainment.

*   *   *

Using the expression "our immediate family" causes me to recall family discussions concerning relationships. In the past I often heard people say "second cousin once removed," or "double third cousin," and I never quite understood the intricacies of such connections, nor am I sure what an "immediate family" is. I was referring to our

160

five children and their children in the paragraph above. This week's scribblings may invite comments about wasted space. I can't say (as an excuse) that I'm suffering from jet lag, since I don't fly, but I have had a bit of reaction caused by making two rather hasty trips to distant places within the last two weeks. Perhaps I should move from being semi-retired to a state of total retirement, but I doubt that I will, willingly.

*   *   *

Hearing someone mention the difficulty of transporting all the bags and baggage, including necessary equipment, such as stereos, when students are being taken to college, will almost invariably cause older bystanders to recall how different it was when students went off to school in the past. I'm guilty of such thoughts, recalling the one hatbox and the cardboard boxes that accompanied me to Marshall College. Of course, that was long, long ago, and I blush to recall the number of dormitory elevator trips needed when our younger daughter first enrolled in Concord. How, exactly, did we reach such a stage? Our daughter had earned the money to buy the extras she considered essential. Should we have told her what to use the money for? Can we blame the general state of civilization for causing students to "need" radios, tape players, etc.?

☙ July 22, 1993 ☚

I have heard people speak of "a mixed blessing." I suppose they refer to something which has bad aspects in addition to good. After approximately 45 years of keeping house, I have finally succumbed to the temptation to say, "OK, let's try air conditioning, which I consider a mixed blessing." I have given notice that when temperatures are lower I'll want to turn off the machines, open the doors and windows. I don't like closed doors, even though I'm very

161

glad I have a door to open. I don't like not being able to watch the chipmunks as I sit at my dining room table, but I know this is a petty complaint and I can look over the top of the bulky contraption installed in the window and see the hummingbird in the Mimosa tree. And, of course, I know I'm lucky to have a table, a window, a tree, and even the mixed blessing of air conditioning. I do think of the cost, the loss of energy, the effect on the world, but I know that cool air can be a blessing, to infants, to older people and to people who must work, regardless of the temperature. Conclusion: Civilization poses questions. And, as I said in something I once wrote and called a poem, "Who brings comfort to the girl who waves the fan over the diners?" I didn't know the answer, of course. I also, mentioned, I believe, the fact that men who make the electricity we use often work in very uncomfortable conditions. I know this from close-at-hand information because my husband worked for several years as a welder and pipe fitter with a boiler maintenance crew, helping to provide electricity for our homes

* * *

A friend trying to adjust in the best way possible to the loss of a family member, says that she has been besieged by suggestions from people trying to be helpful. Their recommendations include suggestions about what she can do in her spare time, and advice about where she should live. For the moment, she wishes more people would realize that she needs to rest. It is difficult to know how to be truly helpful when someone dies, but if people who have experienced the loss know that we care about their feelings, perhaps that is enough and most helpful.

* * *

Someone who came to lunch at our house brought a book to share. Written by Harold Kushner, the book has an intriguing title: *When All You've Ever Wanted Isn't*

Enough. Chapter titles are interesting, too. Examples: "Go Eat Your Bread in Gladness" and "Feeling No Pain, Feeling No Joy." The book is published by Simon and Schuster's Pocket Book division.

*   *   *

My husband attended a Lyons family reunion in Kentucky. (His mother was a daughter of George Washington Lyons). Our youngest son accompanied his father–a good experience for him. While they were in Kentucky they took a side trip to Greenbo Lake State Park which is the location of the poetry workshops my husband and I have attended for several years. I think our son now knows one of the special reasons why I like to go to that particular conference. The lodge is on a hill which slopes down to the lake where my husband fishes. I can easily see him from the lodge and even call him when it is time to go to the dining room.

❧ July 29, 1993 ❧

Perhaps death always comes as a surprise. We expect it; we say we know it is inevitable. Yet, we are surprised when it happens. This may be related to our telling ourselves that accidents happen, "but nothing will happen to me; I'll be careful." In one sense, this is good; we shouldn't go around always expecting the worst. (Of course, all children, young and old, know that all mothers, young and old, think that you should always take a sweater or raincoat when you go out. And you should always have a quarter tucked away somewhere, to prepare for an emergency phone call. Of course!)

Sometimes realization of loss comes long after we have lost a family member as we recall the good things that happened in our relationship. We can remember and be

163

grateful for the good, realizing that very few relationships are perfect. Too, as time passes we can reach the point of forgiving ourselves for our omissions, real or imagined, hoping to "make up" for them as we relate to other people.

It seems to me that the sharpest sense of loss I have experienced occurs when someone I know is suddenly no longer alert and knowledgeable. I experienced this feeling last year when my aunt, during a short illness, was not able to talk with me. Thankfully, she recovered and when I saw her last month she was able to discuss such subjects as a recipe for corn bread and the evening dresses she made for me, a long time ago. True, she introduced me to someone as her granddaughter, but this was a slight lapse, compensated for when she remembered to ask me about the novel which I expect to have published before November.

I am thankful that many older people are able to keep going and going and going, productively and happily. I am thankful that, as time passes, we learn more about how to live with and, if need be, take care of, older people.

Bill Withers, a native of West Virginia, successful enough to have traveled far and wide, says he likes the way West Virginians show love and respect for the elderly. He tells of his duty as a lad, assigned to walk with his grandmother to and from church, sit with her and let her lean on him as they walked, if need be.

Life styles have changed, even in Bill Withers' time, but more attention is being paid to studies of the needs of the elderly. I am hopeful that when and if my arteries and brain cells produce eccentric senile actions that people around me won't attribute my behavior to pure ornery cussedness, but will have learned some facts concerning the cause of my actions. Perhaps someone will give me individual attention, answer my questions, and help me find my glasses when I ask for my teeth. They will be patient because they have learned more about my condition than most of us know and understand today. Come to think of it, I could use a little help finding things most any day of the week, every week!

◁ August 5, 1993 ▷

When we consider that fact that many of the grandparents and some of the parents of adults living today were born in the 1800's we realize that historical people we read about were not so far away and long ago, after all. Nathaniel Hawthorne, for example, died in 1864. I've been reading his collection of stories for children titled *A Wonder Book.* The preface to the book is dated July 15, 1851. I had failed to read his novel about the house with seven gables until not too long ago. I enjoyed it.

*   *   *

I mentioned Ozymandias in a previous column. Since then I have turned many pages in several books trying to find "Ozymandias." I had forgotten that this is the title of a poem written by Shelley (a poem which rhymes, incidentally). I had a picture in my mind of lines about Ozymandias appearing on the left hand page of a book. It seems the picture didn't help a great deal because two of the four copies I finally found appeared on the right hand page of the books they were in.

The fourteen lines of the poem were written sometime during or before 1822. They tell of a king whose statue has been shattered, leaving only a few portions of the statue lying in the desert. Words that remain on the pedestal tell us that we should look on the works of

Ozymandias and despair, implying, of course, that his accomplishments were super-great and therefore beyond the reach of ordinary mortals. The message is thought-provoking.

Contemplating the fact that buildings, statues and other great works crumble and disappear may teach us to put our petty disappointments and relatively unimportant failures and success in the proper perspective. We can be aware, however, that words and deeds live on since what we do and say affects people around us. I think that even our thoughts may have far-reaching results since what we think determines whether we're smiling, frowning, looking angry or peaceful. A photographer said to me once, "Your picture was better this year because you weren't thinking of yourself." That should tell me something.

*   *   *

One of the books of poetry that includes a copy of "Ozymandias" has an introduction by Christopher Morley, in which he says "kingdoms crumble and old buildings are wrecked in dust and splinters, but no one tears down old poems . . . They deal . . . with the real joys and horrors every person knows."

*   *   *

We have heard so much about civil rights issues in recent years that attention to the subject seems to be a fairly new development. It comes as somewhat of a surprise, to me, at least, to learn that the American Civil Liberties Union was founded in 1920 and that Helen Keller was one of the founders.

*   *   *

Speaking of dates and the passage of time, I find it rather amazing that our country is so young compared to other countries in the world.

While preparing cheese cake for a family birthday celebration, I noticed a slight difference between the ingredients in two packages, both made by the same company. Suppose I hadn't noticed the difference in the color of the crumbs, and suppose the difference affected the taste of the crust. If someone should say, "This isn't as good as usual," would I immediately think I had failed? I might wonder if I had made an error in measuring or adding required ingredients.

When we make something "from scratch" that doesn't turn out well, we are fairly certain where the blame lies. Earlier this week when my husband said the rhubarb pie didn't have the flavor of rhubarb pies he ate fifty years ago, I agreed with his verdict and accepted the fact that I hadn't done well. I know what caused the flaw; I added raisins to the rhubarb because two recipes recommended raisins and I made a misjudgment concerning the amount of sugar needed. The pie was too sweet.

I think we can have certain psychological reactions in relation to cooking. I once knew someone who could make delicious meat loaf, but declared emphatically that she had never been able to make a gelatin dessert successfully, even though all that's required is to add water and stir.

I have never been satisfied with my attempts at making homemade rolls. I think this is because the Parker House rolls my mother made ("from scratch," of course) were perfect. It may be that I have tried to hurry the roll-making process, however.

We can have mental attitudes that impede our performances of any kind. A great deal of skill, including perception, is required to nurture aptitudes of children. Teachers who can encourage students to develop latent skills are invaluable, and parents who can convince their children to ignore the hurtful taunts or criticisms of schoolmates are to be commended. I have occasionally failed in this respect. One of our daughters, who has a beautiful singing voice (not just my opinion) gave up when criticized by an associate.

*   *   *

Speaking of music, I like the Lawrence Welk show and I love Glenn Miller's music. I've seen the movie, "The Glenn Miller Story," several times. When the band leader (portrayed by James Stewart) dares to play a "St. Louis Blues" arrangement for the marching soldiers–Hooray! He has defied top brass, but the outcome is favorable.

Speaking of music, the music for my play, "Flowers Grow in Coal Dust," is not bad at all. (Not just my opinion). The melodies were composed by John Marshall and Jim Snyder and orchestrated by Judy Cavendish. Anybody interested in production?

*   *   *

Jack Rosenthal, in an article on language in the *Sunday Gazette-Mail* (Charleston), says, "Writing, whether clear or clouded, freezes thought and offers it up for inspection."

❧ August 19, 1993 ☙

My husband suggested that we send part of the vegetable soup that was simmering on the stove to a neighbor's house. We knew that someone there was recuperating from a hospital stay. I was hesitant, thinking

168

that the soup might not be the best I have ever made. The temperature outside was near 90 degrees. Who would want soup? I had decided to make vegetable soup chiefly because we still have several packages of last year's tomatoes in the freezer. Besides, I like soup.

I tasted the soup again. Although I had put most of the refrigerator left-overs in it, it wasn't bad, so I made a telephone call and the response to the offer of soup was enthusiastic. The next day I learned that the soup was enjoyed, and that, as a matter of fact, the recipients wouldn't mind receiving more soup. So I complied.

I wonder how often we refrain from doing something that would really be appreciated simply because we think our efforts wouldn't be good enough or not really needed. I never feel embarrassed when I send $2 for a cause instead of $20. After all, the cost of postage for the voluminous mailing has to be paid, and the need just might be legitimate. Every little contribution should help. I don't answer all the pleas for help (those that come in the mail from unknown agencies) and I don't think I should, but sometimes I think of visiting or inviting someone, but fail to act.

Now I see that I have mentioned two different kinds of helping, and not very clearly. Someone was kind enough to say my scribbling is thought-provoking. I have hoped that might be the case and I hope that what I write doesn't often seem confusing, as it may when I jump from one subject to another. When I make brief comments I think I'm trying to avoid sounding like a know-it-all, but perhaps this has the opposite effect.

Quite a long time ago, after I had read duNuoy's *Human Destiny*, I wrote a letter commenting on the book and the author's philosophy. My letter was published in *The Charleston Gazette*. A friend of my brother, having read my letter, said, "Shirley, what in the hell were you talking about?" I don't know whether my reply enlightened him. He was not arguing about a point I had made or disagreeing with what I said. He was simply saying that my letter hadn't made sense for him. It wasn't clear, and that's bad. He cared enough about reading to read the letter and it should probably have been written so that anyone could understand what I was trying to say. At this point in time, I don't recall what I was trying to say. So be it.

*　　　　　*　　　　　*

What am I reading these days? At present, Michener's *Mexico*, which, so far, I don't like very well, and Booth Tarkington's *The Gentleman from Indiana*. About a week ago, I finished Helen Hayes' autobiography, and gave it to someone. I have recently enjoyed Anne Tyler's very different fiction and I bought a copy of a Grace Livingston Hill book to send to someone.

❧ August 26, 1993 ❧

It is difficult for me to understand why public buildings, intended for use by the general public, are sometimes marred or defaced by people who will do such things as tear a lavatory fixture from the wall. Quick answers can be offered: "Some people are naturally mean or destructive," or "Drugs are responsible," but it seems to me there is more to the reason than such ready answers provide. There is much that is difficult for us to understand about people around us. It is possible that we never really know or understand people we have known all our lives.

Studs Terkel interviewed many people and wrote abut their occupations, their daily work. Many people work in conditions that we cannot possibly fully know about unless we do the same kind of work. For example, how many people know the meaning of the word *offal* as connected with the poultry industry? Would you like to work with wet feathers or other poultry discards all day? Most of us don't fully understand why people continue to work in such conditions, just as we don't fully understand why someone continues to work where treatment is unfair or where harassment occurs. Speaking of harassment, I don't fully understand why I kept a promise I made long ago to a student insulted by a teacher. (I had promised I wouldn't report the incident to authorities). Correction: I know why I kept the promise, I don't know if I should have. Something else I don't fully understand: why the teacher acted as he did. And at this point, any readers I have may be saying, "So What?"

I don't see anything wrong with trying to understand, but I know such striving and questioning is annoying to some people. As I said, I've been told that I think too much. I've also been called an iconoclast, which doesn't exactly fit the type of questioning I've been scribbling about in this column. I think I'd rather be called a gadfly. (The definition in Webster's Ninth for the word *gadfly* sounds better than the definition in the Ramdom House College Edition.).

* * *

As I sit at the kitchen table I see a neighbor's tree, which seems at least one hundred feet high. The branches sway a little, then grow still. I wonder if anyone ever counted or estimated the number of leaves on such a tall tree. It seems there must be thousands and thousands, and yet, every leaf is said to be different from every other leaf, just as every person's fingerprints are different from every other person's. Amazing.

In June I scribbled, on the back of a poetry magazine which comes to me from Arkansas, the following words which ask a question: Wind moves over the world. Belts hanging on a closet door move gently, swayed by the breeze. Winds blow fiercely over the world. Tall grasses bend and trees break. What are the winds of war? Do gentle breezes grow? Can we not move, all of us, into sheltered coves or valleys deep and safe, away from the winds that kill?

❁ September 2, 1993 ☚

The title of the one-volume collection of the writing of Booth Tarkington that I mentioned previously is not *The Gentleman from Indiana*. It is *The Gentleman from Indianapolis*. It was given to me in 1959 by my uncle. Imagine my chagrin when I realized that during all the years since 1959 I have given it a quick glance as it gathered dust on the bookshelf, thinking I would read it someday and thinking I was seeing *Indiana*. This morning I checked the list I have made of an alphabetical arrangement of books in our biggest bookcase and find that the listing I have boasted about has the title listed incorrectly. (So what, you say? I'm just pointing out that to err is human, and the saying applies even to those of us who think we do pretty well.)

One reason I have neglected the book this long is that it contains two novels which I first read many years ago. One is *Alice Adams*. The other is *Penrod*. I reread *Alice Adams* recently and enjoyed it very much. I'm finding Tarkington's short stories, which I hadn't read previously, a welcome break form reading Michener's story about bullfighters in Mexico. Although historical information about Mexico is enlightening, it is certainly not light reading, particularly the references to and information about early religious practices in Mexico and the problems connected with the merging of cultures.

*   *   *

Many people probably think of how amazed our grandparents or great-grandparents would be if they could only see all the modern developments and accomplishments. The accumulation of gadgets and inventions has been rather rapid during the last 100 years. Some of us don't keep up with the pace–I, for one, but I have managed to learn to make a few things work.

First, there was a Coke machine. For certain reasons I had stayed home very closely during several years. I was not at all familiar with Coke machines. I remember my first encounter. I was in the hall at the University of Charleston, facing a gigantic machine, quite baffled. Finally, I asked assistance of a student.

Next, I had trouble with the automatic stamp machines at the post office, and had to call for assistance. (I wrote a poem about that, saying that people are needed still.) I am pleased to say that I can use the computers, or whatever they are, to help me find books at the library. I had little trouble there. Perhaps I was more interested and tried harder.

Once I wrote a poem about my contact with various machines, calling myself an "odd little body holding a teacup." I'm not so little now, and I drink more coffee than tea. I have an automatic coffee maker in my kitchen, and a bread-making machine, but for the latter I still have to check the directions. I don't have an electric can opener and my

173

91-year-old aunt had to show me recently how hers works. Enough said. However, I think I've been ahead of my time in some respects, but that, too, classifies me as a misfit. I was told once, a long, long time ago, that I should have lived in the mid-Victorian age.

September 16, 1993

It's a little past four in the afternoon, almost time to start preparing dinner, and it's my turn to cook, but the kitchen is occupied by crab apples. They're pretty this year, very pretty–for the most part worm-free, with no bruises because my husband stood on the roof to pick them. Last night I worked some at the task of making crab apple jelly, staying up too late. Today I waited for the kitchen to be clear of diners and snack partakers. (Of course, I read the morning paper before beginning work.) So far, I've burned two pans, and cut one finger, but I do have one jar of jelly. Apples are cooking, juice is draining from the jelly bag, jars are heated and I may fill another jar before dinner.

It's a good thing I didn't marry a farmer; a wise farmer wouldn't have asked me. My good husband knows that I've felt compelled to take some time today to work at sorting papers as an organization has asked me to do. I've answered the phone a few times, talked with someone who wants advice about publishing a literary magazine, and looked for a book of children's games my daughter says her secretary had lent her. I also made a trip to the building we call a shed, where my husband works at carving, to tell him our daughter would like the color of the eyes of the cat he has carved and is now painting, to be blue-green. That trip gave me an opportunity to explain why I still have unwashed crab apples in a bucket sitting on the kitchen floor. And what am I doing now? Resting for a few minutes.

I've made crab apple jelly before, and it was good (not just my opinion), but I may not be as successful this year. My cookbook tells me to remove blossom ends and stems, halve the crab apples and remove the seeds. The apples this year are very hard, and on another page I'm told that if a fruit is hard, I should quarter it and *not* remove the seeds. What's a body to do? [I removed the seeds, most of them.]

Even such a small project as I'm attempting to carry out makes me grateful for a sink and running water. In addition, I appreciate anew all the canning and preserving my mother did, working in a kitchen with a sloping ceiling, using a coal-burning stove.

Hours later: (Dinner was only twenty-five minutes late.) As I expended energy on my jelly-making, I recalled advice my mother-in-law once gave me, good advice for me. "It does just as well to make a little at a time." She was by no means advocating less work. She knew well that days often aren't long enough to get all the work done, and a little wise scheduling can help. Her advice works well with our frozen blackberries, when we have them. When somebody wishes for a jam cake, I can quickly make jam, even in December, using one package of berries.

Speaking of small amounts, my husband tells me that enough apples remain on the tree to make at least two gallons of jelly. Two gallons? Eight quarts, sixteen pints, thirty-two cups? If enterprising ants find my jelly bag and bowl of juice which I have hidden under a makeshift cover, I can replace what the ants have taken, if someone climbs the tree.

❧ September 23, 1993 ❧

I keep old clothes that are not good enough to give away, not suitable to wear when shopping or visiting, or going to the doctor's office. I wear them. Often they are more comfortable than newer clothing. As I adjusted a ragged, patched garment, I wondered how I would feel if I had no other choice. I would probably try to find some means to secure the patches and make the garment a little more presentable, *but*, if I happened to have a needle, I might not have any thread.

We've all probably heard about school children unwilling to dress for gym class because they don't have proper clothing. We can be glad that in some places provision is made for furnishing school clothing, and resourceful parents can take advantage of clothing offered for resale by charitable organizations.

Speaking of resale, our granddaughter couldn't understand why we told her that many of the items she considered for her school's "flea market" were not good enough to offer for sale–a toaster with an unreliable cord, for example, which we're holding for repair or emergency use. (I can't imagine what emergency would justify using an unsafe appliance.) We managed to find a few things she could take for the school sale, including a few books. Students and teachers were combining efforts to try to provide air conditioning for the school building. That was several weeks ago and they haven't yet reached their goal.

*   *   *

I have noticed that many shiny, "new" paperbacks for sale at bookstores are reprints of works published some time ago, revived apparently because of television or theater productions. An example: *The Thorn Birds*. The movie version was scheduled recently on television and copies of the novel appeared on bookshelves. I think this is encouraging. I think it means that more people are interested in reading. In the past, some people have considered it a waste of time to read a book if a movie had been made.

*   *   *

Thinking of saving old things, I remembered two sayings that I suppose you could call part of our family's tradition. One of these sayings I heard my grandmother say rather often. The other, so I'm told by my aunt, was a favorite of the grandfather I've never seen, the one who died before I was born. You might say the two adages represent a conflict of ideas, but I've never heard that discord existed between my grandmother and her husband. The sayings: "Waste not; want not," and "Use the best that you have and you will always have the best."

*   *   *

177

I once wrote an article on old sayings, but it was never published. I wrote it following the suggestion of Harold Gadd who was editor of the *Gazette Mail State Magazine*. I mentioned such sayings as "scarce as hen's teeth." The article didn't quite meet Editor Gadd's expectations, but he was most kind and helpful and published several things I wrote. I considered an opportunity to free-lance quite wonderful. Mr. Gadd's nephew, Steven or Stephen Coonts has written novels which meet Book-of-the-Month-Club qualifications.

◈ September 30, 1993 ◈

Mrs. Lucille M. Willis of Shinnston, W. Va., was interested in my mention of the quotation about lighting a candle. She wrote to The Christophers to ask for information about the source of the saying, which is the motto for their organization. The answer she received stated that "It's better to light one candle than to curse the darkness" is an old Chinese proverb. Mrs. Willis asked me in the note she sent if I have heard that nobody who can read is successful in cleaning out an attic. I hadn't heard that saying, but I can certainly understand it.!

It is most gratifying and comforting to learn that someone has read what I have written. Therefore, it is almost a serious crime to identify a reader incorrectly, but I have committed such an error. About five months after I included in this column information about someone who sent me interesting facts about apples, I discovered, while looking over previous columns, that I called that person Mr. Phelps. The information was sent by Mr. Thayer, Walt Thayer. I tried to call him to apologize, but the Wenatchee, Washington, operator had no listing under his name.

While thinking of the fact that it is impolite, to say the least, to fail to call a person by the right name, I thought of Shakespeare's famous words about stealing names and purses. I looked for that saying in Bartlett's *Familiar Quotations* and found that the exact speech includes the words, "he that filches from me my good name."

For me, looking for something in the book of quotations is similar to looking in a dictionary. Other words than those I'm looking for catch my attention. These words by Byron I find interesting: "But words are things, and a small drop of ink, falling . . . upon a thought, produces that which makes thousands . . . think." The following words attributed to Jonathan Swift I consider amusing: "I'll give you leave to call me anything, if you don't call me 'spade'." Apparently, Menander, who, according to Bartlett, lived from the year 343 B. C. To 292 B. C., once said or wrote, "I call a fig a fig, a spade a spade." Talk about expressions lasting a long time!

*　　　　　*　　　　　*

Addendum, August 31, 1993: Today's mail brought me a kind, pleasing, informative and entertaining letter from Mr. Walt Thayer, telling me not to worry about getting his name wrong in the April 8th column. He says that when he worked with West Virginia boys some time ago they called him "Red." He says he noticed my error, but never gave it a second thought and he still reads my column. He says he can even be called by a name in another language which means Big Eskimo Chief, but he says, "Just don't call me late to the table when there's fried chicken available." Mr. Thayer gave me a new list of fruit trees that grow where he lives, which makes me wish for some of the apples and pears he mentions. Incidentally, I believe he mentioned in an earlier letter that he is almost the same age as Editor Jim Comstock, and I hope I didn't get that wrong.

*   *   *

Addendum, No. 2: It has occurred to me that when it comes to fall housecleaning, I seem to be lighting only a few small candles in a space where a much bigger light is needed.

≺ October 7, 1993 ≻

As I write on September 5, the Charleston Sternwheel Regatta is still in progress. A friend has invited my husband and me to go out to dinner. We've decided not to go downtown. I've had limited experience with Regatta crowds. One year I accepted the Humanities Council invitation to enjoy the Charleston Symphony Regatta concert, listening above the crowd, watching from the Humanities offices in the Union Building. It was nice of the Humanities staff to extend invitations, but I spent part of the evening wondering what would happen if someone fell from a window into the massed crowd below. (I'm the person who can't watch high rise rescue scenes on television.) I also wondered if the people below were having fun–just moving around, with difficulty.

I'm not a great crowd mingler. I like to watch people in the crowds, rather than going along with the flow. One thing I liked best about coming to Charleston when I was young was standing on Capitol Street waiting for someone. I could rest my feet and hear snatches of conversation. I liked carnivals when I was young; I liked to watch the carnival workers and wonder if they were sorry they left home. I have only faint memories of the bazaars and celebrations I attended at Decota on Cabin Creek when I was small, but what I recall of the bunting-draped booths seems more enticing than today's close-packed crowds, and I don't even remember what foods were offered.

180

Two men–a father and son–are on opposing sides in a labor dispute, both taking or having taken active roles. The father says he can understand his son's decision to put first the need of providing for his family. It seems important to consider and understand such a statement and related actions. In addition, learning the history of the work place may help us understand motives and actions prevalent today.

My father worked in coal mines for many years. His small monthly earnings, paid in return for his hard work as a mine electrician, classified him as a salaried man, not eligible to join the union, but he took me once to hear a speaker at a union rally. I don't remember any of the speech, but I can understand why my father was interested. In all the years he never once had a vacation. He worked continually through as many days and nights as he needed to finish important jobs of patching and repairing worn-out machinery. His salary was not increased because of such work. Overtime pay was out of the question.

I recall reading that Eleanor Roosevelt was shocked to find no rest room or separate toilet facilities in a place where women worked. I have also read that people have worked in buildings so cold they had to wear coats. Progress has been made in improving working conditions; undoubtedly unions have had an effect. It may be that all of us are becoming increasingly conscious of the needs of other people. We can hope for the best.

❧ October 14, 1993 ☙

Speaking of changing times, I once lived in a place where it was absolutely forbidden to come late for a meal. As a matter of fact, the doors were locked and you couldn't get into the dining room if you came late. This was at Marshall College in the thirties–nineteen thirties, that is. With three hundred girls to feed, you can see the reason for not catering to late-comers.

I was late a few times. Usually on Saturday mornings, but if I happened to have five cents, I could buy a small bag of apples at a grocery a block or two distant from the campus. I recall buying delicious pale green or yellow apples, more than enough for my breakfast.

Once, perhaps when I didn't have a nickel, I rushed to the dining room with the bangs that were part of my hair style at the time still fastened with bobby pins. I was lucky; I was frowned upon sternly by Miss Williamson (Hope I got her name right), but not sent back to my room. We were required to be fully dressed, and this did not include curls fastened with hair pins.

Today, almost invariably, someone is late when we're having a "company" dinner at our house. (The company, most often, includes all our family, gathering from hither and yon). The lateness is a bit frustrating, but I'm always glad when everyone arrives safely, so this alleviates the aggravation.

*   *   *

Food for thought: Meg Greenfield, in an editorial in *Newsweek*, describes our time as a period when "there is so little bravery available for generous purposes," but "so much bungee-jumping type daring undertaken for no discernible purpose except self-testing or showing off . . ." She had written commending a successful rescue effort.

Sue Bender, writing in *Plain and Simple* (Harper Collins, 1991) says, "Not knowing, and learning to be comfortable with not knowing, is a great discovery." That reminds me of someone else's saying that a bird sings, not because it knows the answers, but because it has a song. I think that's the gist of what's said on a bookmark I have somewhere. But put the way I've stated it, it's not particularly impressive. Maybe there are too many words without answers, but keeping silent is not always good, is it?

I once wrote a poem, one I've mentioned before, about the two-edged swords of truth being buried under the "whirl of words, that twist and turn and serve a purpose." That's the poem that covered a whole page in a magazine.

❧ October 21, 1993 ❧

When I was growing up, at our house we ate supper in the evening. It seems to me, although I could be wrong, that we ate lunch at midday except on Sundays, when we had Sunday dinner at midday. In our house now we say, "Come to dinner," when it's six o'clock, unless somebody has been making jelly or doing some other thing that has caused dinner to be later than six.

I'm not sure how supper was changed to dinner for our family–perhaps that's one result of my going to college. At Marshall, girls who ate in the College Hall dining rooms were called to dinner in the evening. Perhaps on Sunday at the college our midday meal was called dinner, because we always had hot rolls and ice cream for Sunday noontime meal and cold cuts in the evening. Indeed, thing were different in those days. All of the girls who stayed in the dormitories were expected to eat in the dining room. As a matter of fact, once we paid our room and board fees, most of us had no extra cash for eating elsewhere.

We were assigned places at tables seating six, and we kept those places all the time, leaving our folded napkins in an identifying holder. Not all of us were lucky enough to have special napkin rings. I recall using a clip-on clothespin with my name written on it. I'm not certain how often we received clean napkins.

Perhaps this practice of re-using napkins, which was probably common practice in the past, helped pave the way for paper napkins. That, and the wish to lighten the task of ironing table linens. Beautiful napkin rings are still available, and I have a very lovely set made of black walnut by our youngest son, but they'll only be used for decoration–someday, when I can locate and launder some presentable cloth napkins.

Thinking of supper and Sunday dinner brings pleasant memories of foods my mother prepared: cream of tomato soup, baked steak (made of a kind of steak stores probably don't sell these days), Parker House rolls, lemon sherbet, strawberry shortcake, and a special one-dish meal baked in my grandmother's big iron skillet (in our coal-burning stove). Pork chops, peppers, rice, slices of tomato and onions, carrots and sweet potatoes made a dish called General Early's dinner. I remember that distant relatives from California came one Sunday unexpectedly and were astonished that Mother had such a wonderful meal in the oven.

Steak Mother baked was ground, mixed with butter, perhaps with eggs, and baked to a juicy deliciousness. I am almost certain no such steak is available because I have never been able to prepare any that tastes like what I remember. And then there were foods my grandmother prepared with loving care–potatoes, for example, cut into tiny squares and stewed or fried as only she and the coal-burning stove could accomplish. Incidentally, we didn't have meat for our evening meal every day. Coal company stores received fresh meat only once a week as I recall.

The margarine we used when I was young was white and came with a capsule to color it. Perhaps some people didn't use the capsule. Could that be the reason an author of books for children writes of a West Virginia family eating bread spread with lard?

☙ October 28, 1993 ☙

Sometimes we are told that we shouldn't be defensive about our state. We should accept in silence or ignore labels applied by people in other states, so we're advised. We should just let our worth become apparent. However, it is difficult not to be defensive. A news article about a publisher, a West Virginian living in another state, says the publisher wants readers to learn that intelligent people have lived in West Virginia. As I read this, I was at first indignant that anyone should see a need for declaring that intelligence exists in West Virginia, and then I realized that one of my goals is to help people become aware of our worth.

Last week I mentioned that a current book for children describes a meal for a West Virginia family which includes bread spread with lard. My family was fortunate because my father was a mine electrician and there was always work for him to do, but I never heard of anyone starving in our community, and if people were reduced to eating lard on bread I didn't know about it.

Coal camp families varied; cooking practices varied. We thought it unusual that a family living near us liked tomato dumplings for breakfast. Children in the community were curious about the outdoor oven built for baking bread in the blacksmith's back yard. The cooks in our family didn't approve of the way one of our neighbors seasoned green beans, but we loved to eat the delicious kuchen bread she made–yeast bread baked with a rich custard topping. Favorite recipes from West Virginia or Kentucky farms, recipes handed down from Scotland, Wales, England, Italy and other European countries were used in coal camp homes. Each family undoubtedly had favorites. Another of our neighbors said that he preferred cornbread made with soda. One small boy who sometimes ate at our home said he was tired of the fact that his sister always cooked "dem old beans."

I know that people who grew up in our community during the depression years, people whose fathers worked in coal mines when work was available, survived lean days, moved on and out into other communities where they owned businesses, became salaried supervisors in plants, and reared families of children who attended college.

*   *   *

One of my friends seems to be somewhat envious of the fact that I enjoy eating. She is a kind person with definite ideas and apologized profusely after telling me that I need to lose weight. I do enjoy good food, and I recall very few encounters with food I didn't like. Once I spent the night with a farm family and had to apologize because I couldn't eat the white bacon (pickled, I think), sliced and fried in corn meal. I was pleasantly puzzled at another farm home when cream served was so thick it had to be spooned from the pitcher. My most embarrassing encounter with food occurred at a most unfortunate time–during my first meal at college. The dessert was plums, of a kind I wasn't familiar with. Since Sunday night meals were more informal than at other times, the serving bowl of plums was placed on the table, along with the main course, and it happened to be near my place. I glanced at the plums and thought they were small beets. I wondered why they hadn't been passed around, and more than once I asked if anyone cared for beets. No one answered, and when dessert time came I found out why. I survived this incident. I am a mountaineer, a West Virginian, and I coped with my failure.

❧ November 4, 1993 ❧

If you've found it hard to understand the conduct of young boys of 10 and 11 in these modern times, as I have, reading *Penrod*, a story about boys growing up in a nice little town in the early quarter of this century, may bring about a better understanding of the nature of boys who are by no means tame little gentlemen. Penrod and some of his friends were required to take dancing lessons, but they found ample activities of another kind–climbing fences, hiding in barns, putting on freak shows, facing and learning to be bullies. They seized the opportunity to make use of a container of soft black tar left open by construction workers, and used it to smear each other and everything else within reach, including a minister's hat–the inside of a minister's hat.

*   *   *

Hearing certain statistics, such as the number of people killed in recent or current wars or the number of children dying from malnutrition almost makes me think it's useless to write–almost, but not quite. James A. Haught's excellently written summary of the history of the Kanawha Valley ("From Mastodons to Multiplexes,") gives us the long view, and reminds us that the growth of civilization is a continuing process. Mr. Haught is editor of *The Charleston Gazette* and the article I've mentioned was in the September 28 paper. Of course, we know that *Hillbilly* articles about our state in the not-so-distant past increase our appreciation of the growth we have attained and the people who have paved the way, making growth possible.

*   *   *

Cracking black walnuts and working at extracting the kernels–not very successfully, since I didn't find my nut pick and used a paring knife–made me think of a story I read long ago titled "Nuts To Crack and Mary Ellen." The story told of two sisters. One worked at the tedious task of cracking hickory nuts. Her sister baked the cake, using the nuts, and got all the credit. This was par for their lives. I think the story was in a collection titled *The Tie That Binds*. I don't remember the ending and I don't know why the story stayed in my mind so long. I don't have a sister, so the story wasn't related to my life. Perhaps the unfairness of the situation bothered me.

I cracked the hard-shelled walnuts with little trouble, using a special stand my husband made–a wooden form with a rounded hollow to hold the nut. He showed me a way to hold nuts so I could crack the shell on one end rather than smashing the whole nut, but I chose not to use that method, preferring to keep the hammer away from my fingers. Remembering the stone hearth in his boyhood home gave him the idea for the nut cracking stand, my husband says. He and his brothers and sisters cracked nuts after placing them in dents or hollow places on the hearth.

My one-volume encyclopedia identifies *peonage* as a system existing chiefly in countries other than ours and pertaining to agriculture in our country. However, the article in *West Virginia History*, Vol. 50, a state publication,

188

discusses the peonage system in the mining industry. Accusations of mistreatment of immigrant workers have been made in this century. I was surprised to find that one such accusation referred to alleged happenings at Kayford and at Acme on Cabin Creek, the community where I grew up. Kenneth R. Bailey is the author of the 1991 peonage article.

𝕬 November 11, 1993 𝕭

Feeling a little less alive while working in the kitchen, I sat down and placed my mixing bowl on my lap. I recall seeing such an action in kitchens long ago, but now I never see anyone sitting with a bowl and spoon while cooking–certainly not on television. (We really don't have room for two chairs and a stool in our small kitchen space, but they're there and we use them.) I was trying out a pastry recipe I found in one of my very old cook books–hot water and baking powder included–so perhaps it was fitting that I should sit with a bowl in my lap.

It seems that we hurry so much more with cooking and all housekeeping than people did in the past. I recall a very interesting remark in a short story I read years ago. Two people were planning to speed up their household chores to prepare for company. One said, "I'll do the ironing." The other said, "No, I'll do it. You enjoy it too much." A funny thing is that there isn't any part of housekeeping I dislike doing. It's just that there's so much of it and so many other things to do. I would never call it boring, but it is somewhat exasperating. And, yes, I do use ready-made pie crusts sometimes.

*   *   *

Words from Booth Tarkington's *The Magnificent Ambersons:* " . . . most of the houses . . . lacked style, but also lacked pretentiousness, and whatever does not pretend at all has style enough."

While enjoying a vacation-in-West Virginia holiday, I had the pleasure of learning that Dr. Ruel Foster of Morgantown reads my Scribblings column. My husband and I happened to be at a vacation spot where Dr. Foster, now retired from his important position at West Virginia University, was vacationing. I am honored by his paying attention to my column. Now I know I have at least four readers–maybe five, perhaps six or seven.

    *   *   *

Yes, the George Edward Campbell seen in the snapshot in the October 14th column, is the husband often mentioned here. He and Editor Comstock, shown carrying books, were in the Webster Springs library attending a Skidmore symposium. I was there, too, but that was so long ago I don't even remember what year it was.

    *   *   *

Words of Eleanor Roosevelt included in *Tomorrow Is Now*, the 1963 book published by Harper and Row: "Either science will control us or we will control it."

    *   *   *

Watching people who are watching other people is sometimes quite interesting.

And yes, I am a bit ashamed of the fact that I begrudge the time it takes to remove clean dishes from the dishwasher. I fail to be constantly thankful that I don't have to feed chickens, or spin yarn or make soap. My mother said that when she was growing up in Kentucky she disliked having to hold corn nubbins for horses (or was it cows?) to eat. I wouldn't like that task, either.

Words spoken by a character in Tarkington's *The Magnificent Ambersons*: " . . . the most arrogant people I've known have been the most sensitive . . . Arrogant and domineering people can't stand the least, lightest, faintest breath of criticism . . . "

*　　　　　*　　　　　*

What do you think would be the result if spectator sports were banned? Would provisions then be made to train every person so that each individual could acquire an athletic skill and thus be able to enjoy a sport individually? If this happened, what would be the effect on people who have sat for hours watching others exercise? Would spectators who now tear down goal posts and begin fights still indulge in battle, even though, after training, they had the ability to skate or swim or run and the opportunity to do so? (I never learned to roller skate. There weren't any sidewalks where I grew up.)

*　　　　　*　　　　　*

A frightening section in *The Children of Men*, a novel by P.D. James (Alfred A. Knopf), tells of the destruction of life and property by a group of young men called Painted Faces, and thought to be Omegas, born in 1995. The story takes places in the year 2021.

*　　　　　*　　　　　*

Homeless veterans of the Vietnam War outnumber by far the fallen whose names are on the memorial wall, according to an Associated Press story.

*　　　　　*　　　　　*

A light sprinkle of snow has appeared in our garden. It is chilly in the house. At least two members of our family have problems for which solutions are not presently in sight. Thanksgiving and Christmas are approaching. Surely there is something pleasant to write about. A person I spoke with yesterday told me that she and her husband have been lucky. They have nine children and at present no serious problems, although most, if not all, of the nine children are grown. That is good news.

*   *   *

Planners expect that one thousand people will attend the November conference arranged by the West Virginia State Reading Council, a branch of the International Reading Association. The three-day conference held at the Greenbrier, November 18-20 will include opportunities for hearing and talking with educators and authors.

*   *   *

Perhaps more emphasis on reading and writing can heal some of the world's ills. I know some people won't agree. They would probably say we need less reading and more action, but they may be people who wreak vengeance on fans of the opposing team. It seems to me that greater understanding, gained through reading, must inevitably help in some manner.

*   *   *

The woman I mentioned who has nine children with no problems is someone I know because we are both members of a book discussion group.

❧ November 25, 1993 ☙

Looking at the top of the hill east of our house, I notice that enough leaves have fallen so that I can see spaces between some of the tree trunks on this sunny November day. This reminds me of an evening years ago when we climbed that hill, the children, my husband and I, looking for a bee tree. I don't recall how steep the hill was, or whether we found the bee tree at that time, but I do know that we went searching one evening near dinner time. We probably still had our prized kitchen stove which

192

cooked things in the oven on retained heat. My husband had observed the route the bees took when they left our yard, and he located a bee tree eventually.

The experience led to my interviewing several people, doing some research and writing an article which *The Charleston Gazette* paid for and published in August, 1952. I was given my first by-line and I was elated. I went all-out gathering facts, interviewing the Secretary of Agriculture, an entomologist, a former neighbor and the State Auditor. I must add that I was not the only one to conduct a careful study. My husband's search was preceded by extensive observation. He prepared a special sweetened substance to attract the bees and watched them patiently when he was at home and not occupied with household tasks.

*   *   *

As I prepared to peel potatoes, it occurred to me that what I was doing might reveal something about my relationship to housework. Instead of simply picking up some potatoes, just any potatoes, to take to the kitchen sink, I considered the number of people I was sure would be present for dinner, and thought about the additional number who might appear. I considered the size of the potatoes and tried to decide whether each of the large potatoes would equal two small potatoes and vice versa. Perhaps other people do this, but I have an idea that many people simply pick up potatoes, any potatoes, peel them, perhaps put some back or get another one or two. Perhaps they do this while listening to a radio or talking with someone, and they may be people who are never late getting dinner on the table.

Describing my method of choosing potatoes is not the end of the story. Once they're in the sink, I don't pick

193

up just any potato. I consider carefully which one I want to peel first. I don't know whether this is ridiculous, but I am never bored by the task. I use a hand-held potato peeler for long, smooth potatoes, but I like to use a paring knife for small, knobby potatoes. This fact and consideration of the amount of time I have enters into my planning, too.

I once wrote a story about a woman's method of peeling and cooking potatoes; she and her husband didn't agree about how new potatoes should be cooked. Writing experts tell us we should write about what we know, but that story hasn't been published.

    *   *   *

Words from Ernie Pyle: The surest way to become a pacifist is to join the infantry. No normal man who has smelled and associated with death ever wants to see any more of it.

December 9, 1993

There comes a time when it seems very necessary to discard clippings, letters, mementos–especially so when some of them are much more than fifty years old, and crumbling. However, the sub-deb pages, about 36 of them, which I cherished and have saved since the 1930s are in good condition. The illustrations in the pages which give advice for teenagers are attractive and the topics appropriate for these times, or so it seems to me: How To Be Popular, How To Be Polite, How To Get Along With Your Family, How To Act On A First Date and Other Dates, How To Entertain. You would think someone almost fifteen might be interested, but my granddaughter didn't seem eager to read these pages, so I've discarded most of them. Perhaps young people these days have already seen everything on television, and don't often feel the need for advice from a printed page.

*   *   *

On my way back into the house, having made a trip to the clothesline which I use occasionally, even in November, I noticed the moss between the concrete sections of the walk. It looked new and fresh and I dislodged a tiny chunk and brought it into the house where I proceeded to inspect it with a tiny magnifying glass, one that probably came in a box of cereal. The magnifying glass served adequately to help me see the tiny separate sections that formed the moss. I looked closely, but saw nothing that explained the mystery of creation. That doesn't keep me from enjoying seeing and touching moss, which has always fascinated me.

*   *   *

Parents want their children to be trustworthy. Because we love them we want to trust them. Is it possible that at times they need parents to be hesitant and questioning? It's easy to love our children, but it isn't always easy to know what we should do.

*   *   *

The persistence of growing things is amazing. When the sun shines for an hour or two, the late-blooming dwarf hollyhock tries again. The double begonia, moved from the sunny front stoop to the backyard shed (not really a shed, because it has four walls and a door) continues to bloom, thriving on artificial light and heat turned on only when someone is working in the shop, which we call a shed.

*   *   *

The time is approaching when I will be able to hold in my hand a published copy of my aforementioned novel, "From Black Dirt." The book is scheduled for release December 10 and may be ordered now from Aegina Press, Inc., 59 Oak Lane, Spring Valley, Huntington, WV 25704.

The cost is $8.00 per copy, plus $2.00 mailing charge for the first copy and .75 cents for each additional copy. If anyone should happen to buy five or more copies, he or she may subtract 40% of the cost.

❧ January 6, 1994 ❧

Written earlier, not this year: Two days after Christmas, while I am cleaning the kitchen floor, I think of the words of a song which speak of coming home. I stop mopping to liberate a wad of gum from the floor near the kitchen garbage can. The house was well-filled on Christmas day, and an excited grandchild or a busy parent may have been responsible for the misguided, discarded sweet. The gum is loosened easily and I continue my task, thinking of those who were here and those not yet arrived.

One who came, physically exhausted from overwork, remains, conceding reluctantly that rest is needed. Another is in the process of trying to hold or restore family life and bring peace to a situation where discord, strife and sorrow have existed. Another, on the verge of leaving home, aiming toward greater independence, hesitates to make the break, having found recently that misfortune can be the cause of a need for help. Another experienced long ago the sorrow of being away from home at Christmas time, harried, fleeing, or simply homesick and bewildered.

And so they come, finding love, change, and admitting that "it isn't the same." Sometime it's a chore to come home—inconvenient, tiresome, disappointing, but often good memories are reinforced and blessings are recognized. Perhaps, best of all, a visit home sometimes intensifies appreciation of what has been gained after leaving the childhood home, establishing new places of their own.

A current commercial shows us a character saying he isn't sure what a platitude is, but he has gratitude. Perhaps it's a platitude to say that we can be thankful that the children want to come home, that they do come home, and that often good memories of home abound. I have gratitude. This year's celebration hasn't been too tiring; the grandchildren behaved well; no one stayed too long; the house was comparatively neat when visits ended, and I have found only one wad of gum on the floor.

I hope our children will always be able to come, weary or not, whenever they want or need to come; and when their childhood home no longer exists, I hope that they, in turn, will be able to express platitudes about "home" with sincere gratitude.

I assembled these thoughts as I finished the major cleaning tasks of the day, and then I sat down to read, to rest awhile, before attempting to write. My reading at this time includes Michener's *The Covenant*. The words I read reinforce my need to express gratitude for our homes, for the kind of life possible today. Cruelty, horror and misery exist, and each day we learn of misfortune, but some of us are fortunate enough to have homes to live in or return to, homes to be grateful for, and I like to think that this is true for a greater percentage of people today than in 1662. So, let the platitudes be heard, and may the homes foster and strengthen, adding to the expressions of gratitude.

Which is worse – or better – knowledge without experience or experience without wisdom? I am concerned about young people who know so many "big words" and have no experience related to those words. Perhaps too often, they do have the experience. Is it necessary that they have experiences in order to gain wisdom? Many of them may tell you, and their parents, that they must be allowed to have experiences. I think I would choose knowledge without experience as the better choice, and yet I would ask deliverance from–and–for teenagers who know it all.

        *   *   *

Either a machine or a person with good intentions removed the sentence explaining that my January 6th column was written several years ago. I didn't find any chewing gum on the floor this year at Christmas time.

        *   *   *

A friend whom I've never seen or talked with face to face is a writer and a staunch supporter of West Virginia writers, including me. His positive reaction to my writing causes me to wish that my efforts had produced better work, especially so since he tells me by letter how far his reading of my novel has progressed. This illustrates a point I have made when talking with beginning writers. I tell them that they should send out manuscripts early because when they realize that someone is judging what they have written, then they, too, can look at their work objectively.

        *   *   *

While waiting for half of our asphalt-tile-covered living room floor to dry, I sat down near the bookcase and picked up John Cassidy's *A Station in the Delta*. I noticed the dedication, "To Mother, who listens." This is a rather unusual, and very special, dedication. I read again the high praise given the book by critics in *Washington Post* and

Library Journal and by others. Members of West Virginia Writers, Inc. are fortunate to have had John Cassidy conducting workshops at our annual conferences.

      *   *   *

The reading discussion group which I attend has chosen the book *The Hemingway Women,* for the next meeting. I don't have a copy of the book, written by Bernice Kert, so I'm reading Hemingway's *A Farewell To Arms.* I read *For Whom The Bell Tolls* many years ago. I have wondered if the book which I'm waiting for is about women in his life. I'll have to wait until it's my turn to get the library copy to find out. My desk-top encyclopedia speaks of the author's stunning literary style and says his writing is direct, terse and often monotonous. I recall liking *For Whom The Bells Toll,* but I am not greatly impressed by the "Farewell" writing style. An example of a sentence that doesn't impress me, found in Chapter Two, begins with "The river ran behind us and the town had been captured very handsomely but the mountains beyond it could not be taken and . . . the Austrians seemed to want to come back to the town . . . " Etc. I daresay that if Nobel Prize winner Hemingway were here and a *Hillbilly* subscriber, he would not be greatly impressed by my writing style, either.

ᐊ February 3, 1994 ᐅ

A poet who contributed poems for publication in *Hill and Valley* said that, although much of his writing had been published, over a period of many years, he regretted the fact that he knew so little about readers' reactions to what he wrote. This brings to mind the question, "Why do we write?" Certainly, in most instances, not for money, although a faint hope may always be present concerning those million dollar contracts we hear about. We soon learn that they are few and far apart. Most of us know that we can't even earn our bed and board by writing. Most writers have to have a steady job, probably not even related to writing, in order to earn a living.

Most of us are happy to see our words in print. We know that space in any publication is valuable. But why do we want our words to be published? Why do we put words on paper in the first place? Many people do so and never attempt to see those words in print. They may keep them hidden away, but this is no proof that they would not like to have readers.

When I was in school, in the very early years, when I had an opportunity to write, I wrote because it was fun–writing a story about a boarding school mystery, for example, when I had never been near a boarding school, except through the pages of my beloved Ruth Fielding books. When I reached the tenth grade I had an opportunity to enroll in a journalism class, and I had a few things published in a school paper. I was living with relatives, far from my Cabin Creek home, and my uncle was a member of the faculty. I was shy, but I wanted people to realize that my uncle was not responsible for any accomplishments of mine, so I wrote.

Many years later, one of my first published and paid for articles grew from my frustration resulting from trying to be a perfect housekeeper while taking care of small children. I gave the article the title "Breakfast Was Never Thus" and in it I expressed my chagrin because women in magazines were always elegantly, daintily dressed and groomed, even while cleaning toilet bowls. A few years earlier I had put words on paper about what I considered my failure as a housekeeper, but I sent those words in a long letter to one of my college professors, a Classical

Language teacher. I even told her of a day when my pail of scrub water was left neglected in our apartment living room all day long. The professor was not married, had probably never taken care of children, and perhaps had never scrubbed a floor, but she sent a friendly reply. My putting words on paper had helped, although I still felt a need to write about the problem sometime later.

Do we write for escape? Do we write to solve problems? Do we write simply for the satisfaction of putting in our two cents worth? Why am I writing this? I really don't know, but I know that writing is satisfying. In *The Hemingway Women*, Martha Gelhorn is quoted as saying that the beauty of being young is that you believe you can make the world a better place. She was a writer. Perhaps some of us never grow up enough to give up this dream.

❧ February 17, 1994 ☙

W ho in the world discovered that if someone exerts a little extra energy beating egg whites the result is a snowy, delicious topping for pies? What caused a cook to separate the yolks, anyway? Trying to please a finicky eater?

*   *   *

My husband manages and fills the bird feeders and knows the habits of the squirrels in our yard. Usually, I just look at them occasionally. However, when I opened the door on a cold Saturday morning to see if the mail had come, a friendly squirrel looked at me expectantly. A day or two earlier we had observed a squirrel working very hard at reinforcing the nest in the top of the pin oak. "Probably," I thought, "this is the squirrel that struggled to tear the rope from the rose trellis and carry it up the tree. Such industry needs rewarding." I hurried to get a few shelled nuts from the kitchen, placed them on the step, and watched as they were neatly devoured. This squirrel looked well fed–cuddly, in fact, but it seemed I was being asked for more, so I deposited two hazelnuts, still in their hard shells, on the step. These were inspected then quickly buried at two different places in the grass. I hope the squirrel isn't allergic to salt because the peanuts he/she ate were salted.

*   *   *

What is the origin of the code that says you don't tell on your friends or anyone? It seems deplorable that conditions today cause teenagers to say that they would be in danger of getting "beat up" if they report misdeeds or rule-breaking in junior high school.

*   *   *

One of the very little problems of modern, every-day life: When you have a pen and paper ready to take down a phone number or name or message, the person who is to give you the information pauses for a long time and then says, "Do you have a pencil?" Then, of course, there are those other times . . .

*   *   *

I've finished reading *Convictions*, a well-written novel published by William Morrow and Co. in 1985. The author, Taffy Cannon, gives us a serious picture, reminding me vividly of the 1960's, when stern, steely-eyed FBI men questioned mothers, fathers, other relatives and friends of young men who were conscientious objectors. Those were the days when tracks in the snow near a utility pole might mark the night-time post of someone hoping to be on hand if a wanderer tried to rejoin his family at Christmas time.

*   *   *

An interesting remark about poetry, attributed to Mary Oliver, poetry judge for *Yankee* magazine: "Blessed be the poem-maker, for in the work itself is the spirit's best reward." I have been known to say that the person who

202

benefits the most from poetry is probably the person who writes the poem, no matter what the form is. So it seems that Ms. Oliver and I agree. She, however, is a Pulitzer Prize poet.

❧ February 24, 1994 ☙

The amaryllis given to my husband at Christmas is amazing and the blossoms are beautiful. It's amazing because very tall, second growth, tube-like stems appeared and produced enormous new scarlet flowers, all apparently growing from one bulb. My dictionary tells me that amaryllis is in the belladonna family. The plant has been sitting since Christmas on our kitchen table near the sunny window. I do hope that no poisonous pollen gets in our food, but so far we're okay. Only my husband and I eat breakfast and lunch there. Other people eat wherever, or don't eat, so maybe they'll be safe if food prepared on the table isn't affected. Meanwhile, we can enjoy looking at the blossoms.

*   *   *

Last week I mentioned the "discovery" of meringue. Surely someone did discover it and I do wonder how the discovery happened. So many things have been developed for our convenience and we hardly every think about the fact that once upon a time such a convenience or gadget didn't exist. Who first planned and made coat hangers as we know them now? People used to hang their clothes on pegs. A related thought: It has seemed a bit unfair to me that a person who develops a new and better method for performing a task where he works often is denied any future benefits from his invention since the company he works for will claim ownership.

*   *   *

Speaking of work, someone who worked at the place where my husband worked before they both retired has discovered an unusual and pleasant way to remember the people he worked with. Mr. Ray Lively, who lives at Shrewsbury, West Virginia, began planting trees in 1950, one for each friend, family member or fellow worker he wishes to commemorate. He sends pictures of the tree to the individual whose name on a marker clearly identifies the tree. The card my husband received this year (on his birthday, because Mr. Lively keeps tracks of birthdays) shows clearly that the tree planted to honor George Edward Campbell is doing well. A message on the back of the photo explains why trees are valuable.

*   *   *

I have recently watched television presentations of events in the lives of American Indians. The two segments I have seen dealt with the Nez Perc Indians and their Chief Joesph and Geronimo and the Apaches. I am amazed again to realize that encounters with Indians were still occurring when my grandmother was only ten or twelve years of age. Geronimo died only nine years before I was born. It is interesting to me to note that each of these leaders attempted to leave the United States. Joseph was leading his people toward Canada and Geronimo had already reached Mexico when he was pursued and captured.

I found no mention of Nez Perc, Apaches, Geronimo or Chief Joseph in five history texts, including *A Diplomatic History of the United States* and a book titled *The Story of American Freedom*. However, my Columbia Encyclopedia tells me that Geronimo appeared in Theodore Roosevelt's inaugural procession.